THE HAUNTING OF STEELY WOODS

BONNIE ELIZABETH

MY BIG FAT ORANGE CAT PUBLISHING

The Haunting of Steely Woods
My Big Fat Orange Cat
Horror May 2021

Copyright 2021
Bonnie Elizabeth Koenig

Cover image Copyright © "lighthouse" | Deposit Photo

Cover Design Copyright © Bonnie Koenig

My Big Fat Orange Cat Publishing
MyBigFatOrangeCat.com

ISBN 978-1-953363-13-8 trade paperback

TRACI: SEPTEMBER NOW

I nearly died on a toilet in a rest stop just off of I-5 in Washington on my twenty-fifth birthday. Though it's been nearly twenty five years since, I remain haunted by that night.

My life is filled with things I don't do and rituals I have created to keep me safe. My nightmares accompanied me on the long cruise my long-ago boyfriend, Jason, took me on to help me de-stress, and, he hoped, to help me get over it. He thought it was PTSD or perhaps just an overactive imagination. Ghosts aren't real.

But they are.

They are all too real. Just like regrets.

At forty-nine I have remained unmarried and childless. Jason, of course, found someone else, someone sane who could raise the two children he always wanted and could go hiking and skiing and enjoy a wild and horrible action thriller.

This is also true of Matt, the boyfriend who tried to save me. He already had a child, a daughter, but that ended when she started having the same sorts of nightmares I did. He thought it was catching. I worried he was right.

When they left, she was fine, for which I am thankful.

After that, I gave up, mostly, and lived alone. Alone in Charlotte where the sun is warm and the city is large and noisy with energy and people, both of which I hope will drive away the ghosts. So far it has not worked completely.

But it did work well enough until Deborah Ransome came to work at the bank. Deborah was part of the media services department at the large bank where I worked. I was also in marketing, but an assistant to the producer of radio and television ads. Like me, Deborah was from the Pacific Northwest. She had lived in Portland, like I had, though she was from originally from Mercer Island up by Seattle. Clearly, her parents were old money.

My parents had no money, old or anything else. I'd made it on my own, putting myself through school. I had found a great job in Portland when it was just on the edge of fame and desirability. The Trailblazers were in the finals led by Clyde the Glide and Intel in Hillsboro was still a commute through open fields splattered with interesting and unusual places. The Pearl was an up and coming dream for the most part.

Still, Deborah and I had things in common, though she was younger and had come to Portland after I had left and stayed there much longer, knowing it as the sprawling busy city I often read about. I tended to think of the city as becoming too overdone, like a roast left too long in the oven, hardening and dry rather than moist with promise.

Deborah loved Portland. She remained attached to the Pacific Northwest with its evergreens and rain and gray skies that cover the land most of the year. There's something hauntingly beautiful about it, almost magical. A place where anything could happen. It draws me, pulling my heart strings, though my parents are gone and my sister had always had one foot out of state, dreaming of living in a sunny climate.

Sometimes I envy Tessi her life in Las Vegas. How much less haunted could you get with the slot machines and noise and the tourists? The sun shines most of the time, except when you get windstorms blowing up dust or when you get a deluge that causes flash flooding outside of town. It's a different place even than here, but Las Vegas had felt too close, as if ghosts could be deterred by mere geographic distance.

Which meant that the Duncan sisters were separated by most of the US. Traci and Tessi, no longer inseparable as we'd been as kids. Teresa had been Tessi for as long as I could remember. I'd started it, unable to fully say Teresa when I was three. Tess is three years younger than I am and so much prettier. Still, she's practical and not given over to romantic fantasies. And I think that's why when I nearly died and the ghost followed me that she wasn't really able to understand what happened.

It makes me sad.

It also made me feel alone, despite being surrounded by Charlotte's eight hundred thousand plus residents. They were all nice enough folks, sunny and bright like the weather. They can't drive to save their lives, but I'd settled that by living in a condo near the Lynx so I didn't have to brave the roads too often.

That morning, I was finishing my coffee, having gotten to the office early to put together some paperwork. The blinds on my eighth floor window—not nearly high enough to be important— were open and the sun angled politely so that it didn't shine directly on my computer monitor but still kept my back plenty warm against the air conditioner. The feel of the cool breeze of the air conditioning and the sound of its hum remained a steady thing, something you could count on.

Papers lay scattered across my desk, a wooden thing practically large enough for a body. The desk had grown from an executive sized computer desk to this monstrosity as I had found I needed more and more space. No credenza for me. I wasn't that important, though I had my own little office with a window, even if it wasn't very big and around noon the sun hung at an angle in the sky that required I keep the blinds drawn.

Bookshelves and file cabinets lined the walls behind me. Two chairs sat scrunched in the corner lest I have guests. Other assistants had more space, but they didn't have my desk which allowed me to work things through without having to sit on the floor.

I had been doing that, smoothing my skirt trying to sort some notecards around me on the industrial gray carpet when my boss had come in and seen what I was doing. Afraid of an OSHA violation for me having to use the floor, he'd found the largest desk he could and insisted I get it. To him I was valuable, ghosts or no ghosts.

Now it was mine and if it was idiosyncratic, it was no more so than Will's high school band poster or Anson's bowl of oranges that always made his end of the corridor smell like breakfast.

And the desk was a far better idiosyncrasy than being haunted, which was also mine, though I tried to down play that even more than the desk.

But that morning there were no ghosts, not then. My office was rarely haunted. The smell of coffee kept me awake and kept my stomach from rumbling too much. By now, there were probably donuts in the break room. I didn't need one, but I wanted one.

Debating that, I closed my eyes for a second.

The room got chill and my eyelids snapped open. Above me the air conditioning vent sent out a heavier wave of cool air. Normal for our building.

Deborah walked in. She's tall, taller than I am, with thick black hair that she probably spends half an hour ironing to flatness. It looks good on her though, trimmed to frame her face. She's got a gorgeous smile and if her hazel eyes are a little too close set, no one notices because she laughs easily and everyone around her joins in.

That morning she wore a black skirt that fell just above the knee and black strappy sandals with low heels. In September in Charlotte, everyone is eager for what winter we have, and Deborah was clearly ready to dress for it. Her blouse was gray with dark black embroidery and probably cost her half a month's salary.

"Did you hear?" she asked coming in. A black beaded earring poked through the curtain of dark hair.

"What?" I asked. There was such excitement in her voice that I thought perhaps we'd gotten some sort of award for the bank. It didn't occur to me that I'd have known about that before she would have, unless it had circulated in the break room. Even then, someone would have come by and shared.

"Another woman was murdered at Steely Woods Rest stop," Deborah breathed, her voice conveying both horror and fascination. It's interesting how the two seem to go together as if the person who feels those things is both pleased to not be part of it and fascinated to be looking in on the horror.

A chill ran from the base of my skull to the base of my tailbone, spreading across my back with spider-like legs wrapping themselves around my spine. Goosebumps grew across my arms while my mouth dried and my tongue stuck to the bottom of my mouth like a dying fish.

Steely Woods.

Where I'd nearly died.

I was alive only by luck.

Sometimes I wondered if I was really alive or only existing. I spent most of my time terrified and there were odd rituals I had about certain things because of my experience. It wasn't just losing lovers, it was losing a part of myself, perhaps the best part, the part that knew how to love life and have fun.

"Really?" I asked, hoping my voice was steady. Deborah didn't know about my past. She knew I had lived in the area and probably knew Steely Woods. Who hadn't stopped at that rest stop between Seattle and Portland when a pit stop at the gas station or the next McDonald's was too far to go?

"Yeah," Deborah said. "They're talking about how it seems like someone gets attacked or dies about every nineteen or twenty years. It's really wild. And the women who get killed all sort of look alike."

As if I didn't know. I'd seen the picture of the woman killed a few hours after I'd left that stop. I'd been visiting my friend Ronette and she'd called, frantic to make sure I was okay, immediately noticing the resemblance. The dead woman's hair had been cut almost identical to mine, a short dark bob that curled away from my face. We were of a height and the shape of our faces could have made us sisters if not twins.

They'd compared her to a photo of a woman killed at the rest stop back in 1980. That woman's hair was bigger, curled a bit more energetically, her jeans cut differently, but she could have been an aunt, or give her a makeover, another sister. Who knew there were so many of us?

"Like a serial killer?" Again, I hoped my voice didn't shake, that Deborah didn't suddenly recognize how much like the dead women I looked. Because what would I say then? It's been hard enough to tell the men I had loved or to tell Tessie about what I'd gone through. I remembered their sadness that I'd had such an experience, their disbelief when I described exactly what I remembered happening, moment by moment.

"Have to be a pretty old serial killer don't you think? I mean there was a girl in the early sixties and the one in 1980, the one in 1999 and one this year. If he started in his twenties, he'd be eighty or so now," Deborah said. "Besides, what's up with the time gap? There aren't any other rest stops where women get killed on a regular basis, even if it's years in between. In fact, if the reporter in Portland hadn't been fascinated by the murders, no one would have put together the timing."

"And it could be coincidence, couldn't it?" I didn't know why I felt such a need to poke holes in Deborah's theory. Maybe because I still didn't want to believe what had happened to me.

Deborah settled on the edge of my desk, which was, thankfully, far enough away that she wasn't leaning over me. That kind of thing always creeps me out—not in the same way other things do but, in a personal space sort of way.

"Everyone always says that but I have a feeling…" Just like that she slipped off my desk and waltzed out of the office.

Having delivered her "news", perhaps disappointed I didn't share her obsession, she was off to something else.

I, on the other hand, wasn't sure my legs had the strength to stand up and close the door.

LUCY: SUMMER THEN

Summer in western Washington, pretty much in the middle of nowhere, meant the only interesting thing to do was watch the cars on Pacific Highway. Most folks worked for the logging companies in the area, and at one time, before he'd died, Lucy's father had also worked there.

With him gone and her mother long dead, Alma and Lucy were on their own. Normally, Lucy loved summers, but this year she dreaded it. At school, she could usually get some lunch. At home, there wasn't much hope of it. Alma worked part-time at the local café, where Clyde Marks, supposedly happily married, liked putting his hands all over her tits. It's what kept Alma and Lucy in any money at all.

Still, it wasn't enough. They'd lost the little house that they'd lived in with their daddy to another family, another logger who needed the space. Now they had a little trailer that Alma had managed to purchase, scraping together money from insurance and side jobs, which she didn't say much about, but which seemed to come with copious amounts of alcohol.

The place smelled of cat urine, cigarettes, and cheap spilled wine, which Alma drank too much of. Clyde Marks would come by every Sunday morning when his wife was at church and Lucy would cover her ears listening to him with her sister in the big lower bunk where the springs squeaked and the trailer rocked as if a windstorm raged outside.

The last time he'd been there, he'd seen Lucy and smiled at her. "Maybe you'd like a ride too," he'd said. His teeth had always been shiny white, but in that moment the sun seemed to glint at Lucy and she huddled back against the far wall, which made him laugh.

His boots pounded against the flimsy floors and out the door, which shut with a bang.

"Next week, ya'll get out a here before he comes," Alma said quietly, looking at Lucy.

Lucy nodded. She saw no fear in her sister's eyes, instead something calculated glinted. Whatever it was, Lucy didn't like it. In fact, at that moment she was almost as afraid of Alma as she was of Mr. Marks, though she couldn't have said why. Alma was just trying to keep her safe after all.

The woods around the trailer were thick and dark, the evergreens cuddling each other and keeping the ground plants to a minimum. Lucy and Alma didn't own that land. In fact, the place was where the previous owner had dumped the trailer. They both hoped no one would find it any time soon or they could be forced to leave their humble home.

The little town, which included the café where Alma worked, a grocery store, and a gas station, and not much else was nearly an hour's walk. You could usually hitch a ride to a bigger town and get the mail if you needed to, at least Lucy could. Alma usually sent her on those errands once a week. Lucy liked Wednesdays because Mrs. Pinterstock went into Kelso and got her mail and she'd always take Lucy along on her errands, talking to her like a real person with real interests and someone worthy of dreams, which was more than Lucy could say about anyone else.

Once she'd taken a ride with Jet Evens and he'd tried touching her breasts and when she'd said no, he'd driven in angry silence and left her in Kelso so that she'd had to walk home. Fortunately, Danny Rhoads had seen her and taken her into town. He probably would have demanded a touch or a feel, too, but he'd passed out with his foot halfway on the brake and sent the truck into a ditch. Lucy only had a few scratches and a lot of bruises from the incident and her left knee complained as she walked through the tall grass and into the woods along a path that only she knew and which eventually took her to the trailer.

Alma hadn't been home because she was closing at the café and for that Lucy was thankful. She was in bed before her sister got there.

Mostly Lucy stayed in the woods, afraid of what might happen to a girl in town who had no father and whose sister was clearly willing to do whatever it took for a little money. Lucy herself didn't know what else she might do but she wanted to put off the life her sister led for as long as possible.

She shuddered thinking about it as the door slammed behind Alma while she went out to wash up. How much longer could they go on like that?

TRACI: SEPTEMBER NOW

I huddled in my office, pulling on the sweater I kept hanging over the back of the chair. I had scooted the chair back so that the sun hit me more completely but my body remained encased in ice, the sun not able to penetrate the depths of my core where the ice had formed. The chemical smell of industrial cleansers made my stomach turn.

Around me I heard keyboards clacking, heels tapping, and voices murmuring. Outside, horns honked and brakes periodically squealed. I think that people in Charlotte should learn to use their brakes and gas pedals a bit more gently, but that was just me. I mean, I can speed with the best of them—hadn't I made Portland from halfway to Seattle in under an hour one scary, dreary night nineteen and three quarters years ago?

I crossed my arms against my chest both to warm myself and to control the shivers and shakes that worked their way through my body. Deborah's news shouldn't have terrified me like that. I mean I was thousands of miles away from

Steely Woods, across a very large river called the Mississippi. I should be safe.

Don't laugh. When I knew I had to leave, when I couldn't concentrate any longer on anything but my terror, I had researched the ways to protect oneself from the paranormal. The dreams I had in my apartment in Portland were so real I felt as if I were back at Steely Woods. Once I found damp footprints in the hallway walking towards my bedroom.

That had done it.

Vampires weren't supposed to be able to cross running water and it seemed like that was true for a lot of spirits. So I made sure to put at least one big ass flood of running water between me and Steely Woods. The Mississippi. I wasn't taking any chances that the Columbia ran the wrong way (I was below that too) or that the Rio Grande had mostly dried up or that the creek beside a house was too narrow. No. I would have no loopholes for ghosts to come after me.

It was one reason I didn't go to Tess in Las Vegas. It wasn't far enough, but it also wasn't past some running water. I think if I hadn't had all my confidence ripped from me by the thing at the rest stop, the thing I fled from because I was lucky enough to have been rescued by a pair of teenagers needing to pee, I might have fled to England. After all, it was a fricking island, past the Mississippi and beyond the great Atlantic. How much harder would it have been to be followed there?

I still think about it, though. Running to England. If my bank ever needs someone to go to their London branch and work, I'm on it. I'd put my name in for one such position, but it wasn't in marketing and I'd no experience in any other division so I wasn't chosen. Instead, I was still in Charlotte where the sun shone regularly and the skies were nearly always blue and it was hard to picture ghosts in the new apartment complex where I lived, or in the homes that were building up on the west side near the airport that seemed to grow and expand every few years.

Charlotte was growing. It was alive.

I was inside that aliveness, though I remained half dead.

When I stopped shivering, though I was still cold, practically fast frozen deep inside, I pulled the chair slowly back to my desk and tried to focus on work. It was hard to work through details of planning radio spots, but fortunately I was an assistant and much of my work was organized previously so I only had to follow written instructions. Thankfully, that was all I had to do throughout the early hours.

At lunch time, I felt I was far enough ahead that I could go out and grab a bite to eat. My boss wasn't a task master or anything, but keeping people at bay meant I often ate at my desk, door closed.

"Hey!" Deborah smiled brightly as she met me at the elevator, Will in tow. Will smiled shyly at me, his head down so that he appeared to make eye contact with my breasts. I knew better. Will was too shy to look anywhere and if you asked him what he was looking at, he'd have turned red as a beet.

"Hey," I said. I was trying to think of an excuse to go back to my office.

"I was just telling Will how you were from the same area as I was and had probably been to Steely Woods Rest Stop." Deborah didn't stop smiling, as if that was something to be proud of or joyful about.

"I am," I said.

Will nodded. "I was reading about it after Deborah told me. They call it the haunted rest stop."

Now that was new. I wasn't sure what to say. I mean I knew it was haunted, but I didn't think others thought of it like that.

Another nod. "No other rest stop has such a history of women dying there. And no one knows who kills them."

"I can't believe it. I've stopped there, I don't know how many times," Deborah said. "You'd think there would be warnings. It totally freaks me out."

If she were freaked out, she'd feel like I did, arms crossed, shivering in the comfortable coolness of the elevator. But no, she was smiling and moving easily, not a fearful cell in her body. Even Will seemed more freaked out than she did, but perhaps that's because Will always seems a bit freaked out.

I was glad when we reached the lobby. Maybe Deborah would let me go and she'd stop talking about the rest stop.

"Are you eating? We should all go over to the deli," Deborah said. "Come on."

It was hard to refuse and I lacked the social skills to do so with any grace, so I followed her out, trailing slightly behind her and Will who continued discussing the inherent dangers of rest stops for women, whether they were haunted places or merely great hunting grounds for serial killers.

"I read this book where a serial killer only hunts at various rest stops. That way he kills in many different states and jurisdictions so no one really knows he's a serial killer," Will said. "I forget who wrote it. I read so much and can never keep authors straight."

Deborah nodded. "It's a great premise. It would be really easy if he were a truck driver, too, because he'd have reason to be all those places."

I tried to tune them out, tried listening to the low classical music that played in the background, real Brahms and not something from my teen ears played by violins. Other people were talking about normal things, how the burgers at the bar across the way were bigger and cheaper than if you went down the street to a place that was trendier.

Other people were talking about loan interest rates and

the crazy woman who came in demanding to be given a low interest loan for a new boat simply because she needed it for her husband's birthday.

I'd have loved to be involved in a normal conversation like that.

I relished the sun outside, where it was warm and wonderful and if I stood in the bright light, unencumbered by shadows long enough the warmth might burn through the chill that had infected my core. Sadly, Deborah was walking too fast, and the traffic signals were with her. I returned to the shade of a building all too soon.

Behind me, a car honked. Another chugged exhaust which made the whole sidewalk smell of dead coal. I coughed lightly. At least the sounds kept me from having to answer anything Deborah said as she talked, her arms waving around, nearly hitting a man in a gray suit walking the other direction.

I brushed by a slow moving woman in a brown dress that hung low on her thin frame and then moved around an equally slow moving man in shorts and shirt sleeves.

Finally, we reached the deli where the usual line snaked outside the door. Their sandwiches are amazing, but the wait takes some time. Because of that, people usually took sandwiches to go, so I knew there would be a good chance we'd be able to snag a table.

I pushed through the door, the dim inside light meeting my eyes. I got a glimpse of one of the workers. Behind her, a pale skull, a few strands of hair standing up on end.

Bile rose up in my gorge.

A normal person would have stood up taller, trying to see what they thought they were seeing.

I knew all too well.

My haunting had found me that morning. Sometimes she

did. Sometimes she didn't. Always in nightmares. Only rarely, when I was particularly upset, in day-mares.

I backed up, not wanting to go in the deli.

"Traci?" Deborah said concerned. Will held my arm, perhaps thinking I was falling backwards. I could have been.

"I need to go," I said. "I don't feel well all of a sudden."

I didn't give either of them time to react. I turned and hurried back to the office. I paused for a moment in the bright sun. I didn't seem to be haunted in the bright light of day. The dead prefer the shadows, night time, or dark and cloudy days where they can creep along the edges of life.

I breathed in and out. I was no longer hungry.

A tall woman carrying a briefcase brushed passed me so quickly and so closely that I was turned nearly completely around. Now I was facing the way I had come. I turned back to my office before any skeletal faces could peer out at me through a shadowed window and went inside.

TRACI: SEPTEMBER NOW

I tried to stay in bright places for the next few days, becoming lizard-like in my need for light and sun and warmth. Due to my inability to get warm, I huddled in front of heaters when I could. I made sure every light in every room was on, adding some electric lanterns around my apartment for the places where lamps and overheads weren't quite bright enough.

I had a clear plastic shower curtain so that the shower wasn't darkened in the least while I washed in water so hot my skin turned a particularly unflattering shade of fuchsia before I finished. But the warmth helped. It calmed me a little, relaxed my muscles marginally, though my heart continued to beat too fast.

I take medications for anxiety. I also have some for hallucinations, which, sadly, made my experiences worse. Almost as if in attempting to change the balance of my brain chemistry, I became more susceptible to the spirits, exactly the opposite of what I needed and wanted. When things like this happened, though, no medication was enough.

My nightmares came back, although I was never certain

if they were really nightmares. I'd dream I woke up in my bed and hear a faucet drip in the bathroom down the hall. I'd huddle under the covers, pulling them up around my chin, hiding from the creature I was certain invaded my home.

Even in my dreams the lights were on, though in my dream they were a sickly yellow with shadows that hovered on the edges of the rooms. I'd cower under my blanket, reminding myself over and over that it was just a dream. Just a dream.

My heart would pound and the room would go so cold that I'd be sure I'd been transported to a giant freezer or perhaps the Antarctic in a storm. I wouldn't look though.

Then I'd feel a pull on my blanket.

Boney fingers would pull against the fabric, curling around the edge near my face.

I'd smell the scent of freshly turned earth.

Usually I'd scream in my dream.

Only then, would I wake myself up, sitting straight up, the room lights on, bright and clear showing me the pale wood of the floors, the dressers in equally pale wood and my bright yellow walls. The semi-gloss paint would reflect light, getting into the corners, keeping even those spaces clear of shadows. The closet door remained closed and I had drawers beneath my bed so nothing could live under there and come crawling out.

I kept the bedroom door open so I could see the light from the hallway, always on. There were no windows in the passage and it was the only way I could make sure no shadows lurked.

I'd look out, but never leave the bed. No matter how badly I might have to go, I never, ever got up and used the bathroom at night. Not when I was alone. If I were living with someone I could see myself going, but only if they knew

I'd be in there. While I doubted they could rescue me from a ghost, having someone nearby felt safer somehow.

Ever since I had heard about the death at Steely Woods, I had had the dream twice a night. I was tired and irritable during the day. I ate poorly, something that is common when I'm overwhelmed. I worried that my work was suffering. I couldn't afford to lose my job, too.

I considered calling a therapist, a different one. I've been through seven already, two in Portland, the other five here. I'd tried being brutally honest about what happened, which got me the drugs. I'd tried hedging, talking about nightmares after nearly dying at a rest stop. I talked about it as if the would-be murderer had been human and not made of rotting flesh, but the therapists always poked and prodded and then gave me platitudes about PTSD.

I sometimes go to an acupuncturist, which, while it doesn't take away the fear, it sometimes allows me to feel as if I can manage it, as if I could be powerful enough to stand my ground and not fall apart upon seeing the ghost or zombie or whatever the hell it was in the rest stop so long ago.

I considered calling the acupuncturist, but I put it off, as I always did, trying to power through the days, attempting to forget about the terror that haunted me.

On Friday morning, my boss, Nils came into my office while I attempted to make sense of a document on my computer screen. He didn't knock, nor did he interrupt me. It's hard to be interrupted when you can't make sense of something. As always, my heart beat too fast and my feet danced around under the desk. My back ached from stress. My eyes burned from trying to focus on the computer, and I both looked forward to and dreaded the weekend.

"On Monday we're taking a road trip," Nils said in his usual quiet voice that somehow seems to carry across vast spaces. He's a large man, both tall and broad. He exudes life force. He is, as one of my counselors said, grounded, though of course she wasn't saying it about Nils. She was talking about me becoming grounded. When she said the word grounded, I immediately thought of Nils. He's like a tall tree in the forest that's stood there for a hundred years or more, roots sinking deeply into the earth, pulling him down and anchoring him to the world.

"Where?" I asked.

"A radio show outside of Raleigh. I'm taking Deborah, Anson, and you along with me. Pack a bag. We're only supposed to be there for the day but they want us to plan for two, just in case. Sandy has already booked rooms at the Sheraton."

Rooms plural, because heaven forbid we have to share with each other. That would require the bank to understand our sexuality and our preferences and they didn't want any sense of impropriety. Which meant I'd be alone in a hotel room. I have extra electric lanterns that I pack for that, just in case. But I still hate it. I can't light up a hotel like I can my apartment, though I try. At least Sheratons typically have good light.

I nodded and tried to smile, like this was all fine. My tapping feet gave lie to that, although the desk hid them from easy view. Maybe Nils wouldn't notice.

The line between my hair and my forehead began to feel damp. My palms were soaking and I didn't dare type anything on my computer.

"Have a good weekend. Plan to be here early on Monday, I'd like to leave by seven. I'll have a van rented and we can all go together," Nils finished. He had a slight frown, probably noticing the sweat. I'd traveled with him before. He knows I'm not a good traveler.

Usually we go by plane. I wait to use the bathrooms on

planes, probably the only person to do so. But I've never been attacked in an airplane bathroom. They're probably too small even for a ghost to share. I feel more comfortable in there, at least mentally. Physically, I'm no more comfortable than anyone else.

I couldn't remember the last time we'd driven, but I knew this wasn't the first. It had been a completely different group and I was new, an assistant to an assistant or something like that, carrying papers, getting coffee, planning the reservations so I knew what I was getting into. I'd talk to Sandy later about the logistics.

Nils left, finally. I stood up and stretched, looking over the city. The last thing I wanted was to leave it, particularly not now, not when I was already keyed up. I could probably get an acupuncture appointment, but there was no way I'd get into a new therapist before Monday. I rubbed my hands down the sides of my pants and then cupped my neck to stretch. My mind raced wondering how I'd get through the trip north.

LUCY: SUMMER THEN

Lucy thought she'd never stop crying. No reason to stop crying. She hurt physically, where Clyde Marks had finally taken her virginity, but worse was the pain of betrayal. Alma had given her to him. Lucy had hidden several weekends in a row between the trees in the woods, laying flat on the ground, her stomach pressed to the cool dirt in the shade of her favorite firs, the smell of loam reaching her nose so thickly that she could taste it in the back of her throat.

Birds chirped and small creatures scurried around her, she lay so still, barely breathing, enjoying being one with the little woodland. It wasn't so bad having to leave early on Sunday, not really.

Except he came Saturday, all dressed up. He'd given Alma money and Alma had smiled at Lucy and nodded once at her and then again towards the sleeping area in the trailer. Dread had spilled through Lucy's back and into her body, filling her until she was frozen in front of the two predators.

Then came anger at her sister who was supposed to

protect her, who was instead selling her to this brute of a man.

"Remember Clyde, her first time! Be gentle!" Alma had sung, leaving the two of them in the trailer, alone, taking the money to do whatever it was she wanted.

Lucy wondered how much it was. How much was her body worth? How much was her trust worth?

Clyde had been reasonably gentle and if she'd had any feelings for him, Lucy had to admit it probably wouldn't have been so bad. But now she hated him. And she hated Alma.

She was back out in her safe place, though it was long past dark and the night creatures were out. Her sobs were quiet so she didn't immediately draw her sister's attention. The night creatures were giving her a wide berth. Lucy could have hoped for a poisonous snake to come up and bite her and put her out of her misery. Clyde might have paid Alma for her but who else would pay her? And what else would they want from her?

Rain started to fall, a light mist that she hardly felt, though soon enough her dress stuck to her in places it shouldn't have. It made the forest smell nice enough, all pine pitch, loam, and a musky scent that Lucy couldn't place. She wasn't ever going back in.

She fantasized that the animals would bring her treats and keep her safe like in her books. But there were people around. It wasn't that wild. The Pacific Highway wasn't far, and sometimes if the car wasn't well kept up she'd hear sputtering and rumblings as it passed by.

Lucy's fantasies turned to teaching the animals to kill her sister, to take her and rip her apart for selling Lucy's body. Alma hadn't even talked to her about it, hadn't given her a choice. It was already a foregone conclusion when Clyde Marks was standing in the trailer taking up all that space.

She'd never get decent rides again because people would

know. They'd know that she was a fallen woman like her sister. People would whisper about her and her few friends, those girls that made her feel almost normal, would stop talking to her. Who would hire a tramp like her?

Her life was over, at least as she'd known it. Lucy began to cry again, thinking of all the things she knew she'd miss out on, things she'd never really thought she wanted before. If she was honest, they'd probably always all been out of her reach, but now she knew for certain that they were.

Her sister, the one person she thought she could count on, had taken all that from her. Anger built in Lucy's chest. The red heat of the anger dried her tears and her sobs until she fell asleep beneath the firs.

TRACI: SEPTEMBER NOW

The van the bank rented was a newer model Chevrolet Traverse in an odd sort of gold metallic color. The seats were black cloth, which surprised me. Normally we get high end rentals but perhaps Nils had specified no-frills, which was struck me as amusing, but not enough to laugh. The Traverse was far more plush than my decade old Toyota.

Deborah claimed the front, which didn't surprise me. I didn't argue with her although I could have pulled rank. Technically, I was senior to her. It didn't matter. I hadn't had any coffee that morning as it was a long enough drive that I didn't want to feel I needed to make a pit stop. Deborah had a large plain Starbucks and Anson had a grande something, probably a fancy thing like a macchiato. Whatever he had chosen, it smelled divine and I wished I had a normal enough life that I could drink coffee on a road trip without having to worry about pit stops and communal restrooms that might be haunted.

Nils set the radio to a low murmur of New Age flute music.

"Really?" Deborah asked, taking a sip of her coffee.

I said nothing and waited for Nils to wax philosophical about how relaxing instrumentals were and why he liked them. I didn't have long to wait.

Anson pointedly avoided looking at anyone during the lecture, paying attention only to his phone. I didn't blame him. It was probably all that was keeping him from laughing. I didn't need my phone, I just thought about the hotel room and the fact that there wouldn't be full light in the room while I was there.

I turned my face from the car and looked out the window as Nils guided the Traverse onto the highway. I let myself rock to the sway of the vehicle. The flute music washed over me. Nils continued talking about how he loved instrumentals and new age style instrumentals in particular, except drum music which sometimes got him too agitated. I was practically falling asleep with my eyes open.

Deborah was making the minimal noises one does when one is being polite to someone else. I was glad that she was on the receiving end for a change. Normally she was the one talking too much.

I drifted in and out while we drove north to Raleigh. We passed the rest area near Concord and no one made any noises about stopping, for which I was thankful. I breathed out a little heavier, not quite a sigh as we passed the first one.

We were all the way to Raleigh before we had to stop at all, Nils navigating us to the studio where we'd be working for the day or perhaps two.

The radio offices were in a whitewashed brick building about four or five stories high. Inside, only the reception area had any windows, tall ones that reached nearly floor to ceiling, but the heavy overhang outside blocked part of the light. The lighting for the rest of the building was provided by overheads that didn't do much to dispel shadows.

Beyond the reception area lay a long corridor, much too dark and shadowy. On one side were the booths for regular users and on the other side were the rental booths.

We had a large room, like a conference room where we all got to sit around and hash out what needed to be done, once again, and then there was the booth that would hold the three voice actors who read the script. The rest of us would be crammed in the room where the sound mixer worked in order to see them work.

While clean, the rooms held a lingering phantom odor of cigarettes and stale coffee. The smells did nothing to improve my mood, which was always dark when I was forced away from natural light. I felt particularly bad that day.

Arguments broke out over things that had been set days ago. I noted changes that were wanted in the script, making sure keywords for our marketing campaigns weren't erased in the ensuing discussions.

I nibbled on a scone and regretted it. It was a lovely pastry filled with cranberries and drizzled with an orange glaze but it made me thirsty. Thirsty meant drinking water or coffee and doing so would require a trip to the bathroom. As it was, I was more aware of my bladder than I wanted to be.

I hoped that the studio was small enough that the bathrooms would be private but I had no way of knowing whether that was true. I nibbled some more at the scone. It was tasty and perhaps the dryness in my mouth would overcome the pressure in my bladder.

Nils and the director went over the script. Nils decided he didn't like the voice on one of the actors. It was too similar to another actor and he wanted distinctive voices, showing a diversity of people. He wanted someone with a bit of an Appalachian accent and then someone with no accent at all. Given his slight southern drawl, I wondered if he meant a voice like his or one like mine.

I took notes halfheartedly.

Lunch came along. I was disappointed that we weren't going out. Deborah was on the phone, making calls, ordering food in. Nils listened to the audition tapes various voice actors had sent in on the computer.

Anson made drawings as he read through the script and heard the actors talking. He'd make print ads that used the same keywords and utilized graphics of what the conversation setting made him think of. Granted, the script had a setting but it was fairly generic. Anson had the task of putting visuals together

I kept busy taking notes for Nils and following up with the people back in the office. I looked through our ad purchases for the last month with the new keywords we were targeting and checking into the return on investment versus older keywords we'd targeted previously. I made a note for Nils about one of the words that had had a good start but was no longer generating any interest.

We discussed that.

Deborah came in with lunch. She'd gotten Chinese and it included cups of soup. I was definitely going to have to find the bathroom.

We all ate at the table, which was far too cramped for a group of our size which, in addition to our lunches, held papers and computers from our work. I held my elbows in. Anson closed his computer for the moment. Even the voice actors got lunch. We shared around the fried rice, Kung Pao chicken, and garlic string beans. You can get better Chinese in Portland, but this was better than many places in Charlotte.

Soon enough I could wait no longer or I'd be paying more

attention to my body than to Nils. I went in search of a bathroom.

The narrow hallway felt dark and cramped, though the walls were painted cream. The length and lack of light made me feel like I was walking through a tunnel on a rainy afternoon. I thought about the men and women who had to push equipment down this corridor and felt for them. Really, though, I felt for me, given that there were bulbs only every four feet and far too many shadows. An industrial gray carpet looked black in the dimness.

Any discussions that might be taking place in other rooms were hidden by the sound-proofing leaving me alone with the humming of the air conditioner. If something happened out there, I had little hope of help coming.

The women's room, when I came to it, was an old style stall bathroom with three stalls. Dark brown metal partitions offered privacy, though legs could be seen under them. I ducked down to look under the doors. No one. Behind me three sinks hung on the wall, the far one with a slight chip, a black scar against the white porcelain.

My heart hammered just standing there. My palms sweated and my bladder threatened to not even allow me to make it to the toilet.

I reminded myself that I was safe, probably. Outside the sun was shining, people were walking around on the streets, cars were driving by. There were people on the other side of the wall, probably, and upstairs and down.

No one had died in this building and certainly not in this bathroom.

Logic doesn't work against fears.

Still, my bladder demanded I go. I cautiously took the stall closest to the door, latching it.

I settled on the toilet, hearing the paper I'd set around the edge of the seat crinkle slightly as my weight moved it. I smelled the old smells of cleansers over the stark aromas of bodily functions. I swallowed and allowed myself to go.

Naturally, now fear made my bladder clench. A second ago, I'd practically wet myself.

I closed my eyes and started counting, hoping that would take my mind off things.

I pictured my house. My semi-safe bathroom where there was one toilet and I had the doors open and the lights on, where my clear shower curtain showed me what was in the tub, which was always scrubbed clean so that no shadows marred my view, particularly if I were only half awake.

Finally I was able to go. I almost sighed with relief.

My pants were pulled up, the button being fastened when I heard the single drip of a faucet.

Bile rose. My heart threatened to hammer its way out of my chest like the creature in the movie Alien.

My palms heated up even as my fingers shook so hard I could hardly fasten the single button.

I needed to get out, but if I left, I worried what I might see.

I heard the creak of a door from the stall down the way.

I pressed my back against the cold divider.

Tears formed in my eyes. I wanted to curl up in a ball and hide, but there was no hiding.

My nightmare had returned.

Time stretched. I listened, straining to hear whatever was coming towards me get closer, but my ears picked up nothing.

My lungs strained.

I drew in a shaky breath, trying to be quiet but unable to do so.

The door to the hall opened.

"I can't believe this," a woman's voice said. Unfamiliar.

Probably from another studio on the floor. There were a total of three of them

I breathed out easier than before. I buttoned my pants, though my hands were still shaking, my fingers curled into claws, still, though now I could use them.

I slipped out of the stall, hoping the other women were in too much of a hurry to notice the tear tracks on my face.

I washed my hands.

Splashed water on my face, drying it quickly.

I didn't want to look like I'd been in there crying. If I looked too bad even Nils would start to question me and Deborah would never let the subject drop until I came up with something to appease her.

I didn't look too long in the mirror, There was a shadow behind me, like the faintest outline of a skull.

I hurried out, not willing to look at that faint shadow too closely, just in case it wasn't just my overactive imagination.

TRACI: SEPTEMBER NOW

I made it through the rest of the day but as I had feared, particularly when even lunch was in the studio, we were running late. Nils couldn't find a voice he liked. He got like that sometimes, never quite getting the exact pitch or intonation that he wanted. Either the voice actors sounded too Appalachian or didn't have enough of an accent. I caught Anson rolling his eyes once and even Deborah started to slam things around.

The day ended only an hour late and we headed back to the hotel in Nils' van.

"I'm just going down to the hotel restaurant," Nils said. "If anyone wants to go out somewhere else, you all can expense it. Just don't go overboard."

The Sheraton was tall, modern, and brightly lit in the lobby. It gave me hope. Music played from a darkened corner where they had a bar, which appeared to also serve food. The tables were spread out into the lobby, separated only by a black rope held up by gold poles. Three women and one man all in white shirts and black vests stood behind the huge black faux marble check in counter.

Two were helping people holding luggage. The other two were talking. Nils walked up to one and waited to be greeted.

I looked up at the large chandelier in the double height lobby. I saw a sign pointing to elevators around a corner. Another sign said restrooms down the same hallway. I smelled nachos, and my stomach growled.

"I might just stay here," Deborah was saying. "I don't really know Raleigh and don't want to wander into the wrong neighborhood."

As if the bank would put us in a place where we'd be in danger. But I wasn't about to tell Deborah anything like that. It would probably start an argument and give her an excuse to start talking about the wonders of Portland. That would allow her to bring up the dead woman in the rest stop up the freeway from there, which was not something I was eager to talk about.

Nils gave us each our keys and then we headed up to our rooms. Nils was on the eighth floor. Deborah was on the third. Anson and I were both on the sixth, though we appeared to be at opposite ends.

"They could have put us a little closer together," Deborah complained.

"We get what we get," Nils said. "If Sandy doesn't specifically ask for rooms close together, we're usually all over the place. It's not like we're family."

Deborah snorted and let it go.

"What about you?" Anson asked, looking at me. "Are you going to come down and join us for dinner? I was thinking maybe half an hour so we can get unpacked and check things out."

"Probably," I said. "I'll check out the room and then head down."

"My plan," Nils said. "We'll save seats if everyone is coming."

I didn't want to spend too much time alone with Nils. I hated having to make small talk with my boss. He liked learning about his employees. I appreciated the interest he took in us but I didn't want to have to field more questions about my past, particularly if Deborah mentioned the murder at the rest stop to him.

The elevators were mirrored above and black everywhere else. The mirrors reflected every trace of light making the little box much brighter than I normally would have expected. Everything boded well for a good night in the room.

The sixth floor was done in blues and greens, bright enough to be cheerful but not so bright as to be garish. The cream walls were covered in blue and green wallpaper done halfway up to a chair rail in white wood. The carpets were the usual speckled blue and green hotel carpet that can be mistaken for nothing else. There must be a warehouse full of that stuff or a manufacturer that makes it just for hotels and other public institutions, always slightly oddly patterned so that buyers can spend hours trying to decide which was least likely to offend their best customers.

I held my keycard near the scanner on the cream-colored door, and it unlocked easily. Inside I found a typical hotel room with a narrow hall near the door opening into a wider room beyond. While the drapes were open towards the back of the room, it was nearly dark outside so the room itself remained clothed in shadows.

I turned on the light which was a bright overhead in the short entry. I was thankful for that. I walked in, dragging my overnight case, turning on the lights in the bright white bathroom. The lights over the sink came on first followed by the lights back where the toilet sat across from a shower. The cream tile of the shower wasn't as reflective as white but it would do.

In the main part of the hotel room, I found a lamp, a desk light, and two lights on either side of the bed. There was also a set of lights over the bed. I found switches to work all of them, turning them on, brightening the room. I opened my small overnight case and pulled out my two electric lanterns and set them out strategically. As I did that, I found a small light over the microwave which sat on a counter over the refrigerator.

I surveyed the space once I had lighted the room as much as possible. A few shadows still lingered in corners, but they were small things, manageable on a normal night. I sighed. Hopefully it would be enough and I could sleep, though my stomach twisted itself in knots.

I'd had so many nightmares right after my near death experience. I dreamed of the creature coming after me and when I dreamed about it, my home had always been dark. Just when I'd begin to think I could turn off a few of the lights I'd have the nightmare again and I'd remember why I always slept with everything on.

The hotel bedspread was white, as were the sheets which helped brighten the place. The mustard colored chaise lounge next to the window did nothing to help, the rather ugly color almost eating the light. Even the black desk chair and espresso wood desk had more shine. At least the walls were cream, like those out in the hallway. The carpet remained the same as the carpet in the hallway, the darker blues and greens creating crawling effect and a few trailing shadows, but at least those shadows didn't move.

I went to the bathroom to wash my face and pull a comb through my hair. No skulls appeared in the mirror nor did the faucet drip, just once. I could even use the toilet there without worrying about what was around. The large glass door of the shower let me see everything. I said a short prayer of thanks to any god who might be listening.

If creatures could come back from the dead to murder the living, then there must be gods too, right? Or perhaps the dead creatures murdering the living was a sign there were no gods. I preferred to believe the former.

I grabbed my purse, made sure I had the keycard and opened the door to go out to the hall. Behind me I heard the faucet drip.

Once.

I froze.

The decision to run out to the hallway and leave everything was tempting, but I knew if I did that, I'd never go back to the room again.

I turned slowly.

The room remained brightly lit. Nothing moved.

The light glowed from the bathroom.

The faucet dripped once more. Twice.

Just a faulty faucet washer. I went back into the bathroom. Played with the faucet until I was certain it was off.

I felt a light breeze on my neck, as if someone breathed on me.

I looked up in the mirror, not wanting to.

The room was darker than I thought.

I whirled around but no monsters waited behind me. Bright white lights gleamed around me. The angle meant that when I stood flush in front of the faucet the room appeared darker, because I caused a shadow.

I breathed out, letting the tension go.

I left the bathroom and went to the door.

I waited, listening.

Someone walked down the hall. Distantly I heard the elevator chime.

Still I waited.

I heard nothing from the faucet. The person above me walked around their room, pounding against the ceiling of my room as only someone on an upper floor can. Were they dancing? Skipping? Or just a heavy walker?

I didn't know. Didn't care. I was glad they were there because that meant I wasn't completely alone.

I turned the knob and left the room to go downstairs.

8

LUCY: SUMMER THEN

Clyde came by several more times, always for Lucy, never for Alma. Lucy no longer cried. Instead, she planned. How she'd get back at her sister who had betrayed her. Clyde never paid Lucy. He paid Alma, leaving Lucy with nothing but pain in her body and anguish in her soul.

"Get used to it," Alma said at the breakfast table. They had cereal, low in the bowls because there wasn't much left. Milk was equally stingy. Lucy didn't care. She didn't have much appetite.

"Why?" Lucy snapped.

"You're a woman. It's what we do," Alma said.

Lucy wanted to scream that it wasn't what all women did, not like that. If so, why was Clyde with them and not with his wife? She wanted to say a lot of things, but Alma wouldn't listen.

Alma would go off and party like she wanted, acting freer than she had in a long time.

"If it's so easy," Lucy said, aiming her barb carefully, "why are you forcing me to do it instead of you?"

"Because Clyde wanted you. He wanted someone fresh. I've got a couple of other men who are interested, too. They'll pay more than Clyde. He thinks I owe him for the job." Alma sneered a bit. "Don't know that I'll have to work there for too much longer though, will I?"

"Why not?" Lucy asked.

Alma just smiled.

The tiny flame of Lucy's appetite dwindled to nothing, guttering in that smile. Her sister was going to sell her body off to whatever man wanted it. She was going to make her money selling Lucy night by night until Lucy was worn out and useless with no will of her own.

Alma ate her cereal quickly and with gusto. Lucy toyed with the stainless steel spoon in the chipped white bowl in front of her. She didn't care if she ate. Didn't care about anything because her life wasn't her own any more.

Girls in school were all having fun, giggling about boys, perhaps getting their first kiss and Lucy worried about pregnancy. She knew then that she'd never marry. Never have her own family. This trailer would be all she knew for the rest of her life, which stretched before her for longer than she wanted it to. What would Alma do if she died?

Lucy toyed with that idea.

Discarded it when she realized she wouldn't be around to cheer for Alma's disappointment when she found Lucy's cold, lifeless body.

She shivered as if someone walked over her grave.

Alma got up, putting her dish in the sink. "I got to work," she said, not turning back to the tiny table where they sat for breakfast.

Lucy would wash the dish later, taking it to the campground and using their sink, which actually had running water. She sighed. Another walk. She hadn't been for the mail in a long time, not that it mattered. But she missed seeing people.

The door banged behind Alma. Lucy didn't look up. She played with her spoon and spun stories about something happening to her sister until she realized not having Alma would leave her alone. Then she wouldn't have any income or food and she wouldn't know how to get an income.

It was then that Lucy began to sob, watering down the cereal in her tiny portion of milk.

She was trapped and there was no good way out of it. Not unless she could figure something out. Some way of making Alma pay.

9

TRACI: SEPTEMBER NOW

Bar food normally isn't my favorite but this was nice, like being back home in Portland where you could get a huge salad or a pizza with artichokes and goat cheese. The pizza had me. Such fare was unusual in the South so I had to try it.

Anson had a burger that was taller than he could open his mouth and he ended up eating it with a fork and knife. Nils had a steak and Deborah had a huge salad that dwarfed my pizza and Anson's burger. She looked shocked when it came in on platter that could have served a full turkey at Thanksgiving.

Everything smelled heavenly, the seasonings of the beef mixing with my pizza, which also had a turkey sausage on it, and the aroma of onions from Deborah's salad. I drank club soda, although Deborah and Nils had beer and Anson had a glass of red wine. I rarely drink because that lowers my guard and it's easier to imagine things.

If my hands shook as I bit into the pizza perhaps it was just hunger. I'd eaten little all day, picking at the Chinese food, dreading the need to use the restroom.

There were other patrons around leaving only three of the two dozen tables empty. A large group sat in a corner, clearly a business outing like ours, but much rowdier. A few tables had couples, two of them men and women and one of two men, who were clearly there on a romantic date, although Monday seemed an odd time for a date to me. But perhaps they were on vacation, traveling through or visiting family.

The dim lights made it feel later than it was and only the noise of so many voices allowed me to eat without fear. I wouldn't have chosen the bar, though there were plenty of people around and easy sight lines to the lobby, which was more well-lit, but it wasn't my choice. I could have gone out, all on my own, and walked some place for a meal but that would have left me to my own devices walking on a dark road lit only by pools of light from street lights. I had no desire to force myself through that. At least in the hotel bar I was surrounded by people I knew and I had found some level of safety in numbers.

Besides, the food tasted amazing.

Deborah held the conversation, as she always did. She expounded on the good points of one of the actors and talked about who she liked for the other voice, though Nils hadn't liked anyone. I hoped he found someone tomorrow morning. Having worked with Nils, I had a feeling he'd call back one of the people and decide they were it. He'd then go on to hate it later, but the commercial would work and, if we submitted, we'd probably get awards. Nils was like that.

Anson managed to finish his burger but there was still a mound of fries on his plate. "I'm not sure I've ever seen so many fries."

"Letting this bar come into the lobby was a great idea," Nils said. He'd finished his steak, which he'd described as being perfect, although a little bit more well done than he preferred.

"I didn't realize it wasn't always here," Deborah said, as if she was intimately familiar with Raleigh hotels.

"Only for a year or so, when they remodeled," Nils told her.

"What made them remodel?" Anson asked. Anson loved hearing stories about buildings changing. It often gave him inspiration for his graphics. I knew that outside of work he illustrated his own small line of comics. One day he hoped to sell it to a publisher or perhaps become his own publisher. For now, his comic was mostly online or for his personal enjoyment.

"I heard that someone had a heart attack and died as they were going through the lobby. Naturally, the hotel tried to keep it quiet, but some cameras had showed the person being wheeled out through the lobby. The hotel wasn't named in the images but the company decided to remodel so people wouldn't be reminded of the incident. Of course, it also gave them an excuse for being closed while reservations were down." Nils leaned back in his chair. He thought it was a good move. He'd have loved to have thought of something like that.

Banks, of course, can't close, no matter who dies in them. Well, a branch could if there were a major crime and a shooting, but the other branches would remain open.

Deborah shuddered and then she smiled. "I seem to be a walking magnet for dead people." She launched into the story of the dead woman at the Steely Woods Rest Stop. She acted like she had been there and witnessed the place.

"Traci would know it too. It's on I-5," Deborah finished, letting everyone look to me.

I shrugged. "I rarely stop at rest stops."

"Still, you were there," Anson said. "That must be scary to think about."

I nodded, agreeing with him.

"Oh poo," Deborah said. "It's creepy but not really scary. It's not like either of us were there to see the killer."

Deborah had never been more wrong. It was on the edge of my tongue to say something, but what exactly could I say? If I spoke about what had happened, people would think I was crazy or imaging things.

"I think it's in poor taste," Nils said. "You act like someone didn't just die, but they did. I can appreciate what the hotel did to cover up a death here but at least they were under-standing. You're acting as if the death at the rest stop were some fictional tale."

At that moment I sort of wanted to kiss Nils. It was the sort of thing I wished I could say to Deborah and have her look nonplussed as if she were shocked that someone would say that to her.

"I guess it does seem rather unreal," she finally said. "It's so far away. Maybe if it were closer, I'd feel closer to it. Now, it's like Steely Woods is something in my past, something I can't believe would happen there. It's a nice rest stop."

She looked to me for confirmation.

"As rest stops go," I said. I didn't smile or say anything else.

No one else did until Nils changed the subject. Still, Deborah's heart wasn't in carrying on the conversation. Anson stayed engrossed in illustrating his napkin and I'm a poor talker at best so the evening wound down.

I left first, pushing my chair away and setting my napkin on the table. We had long ago signed our checks and the black folders lay in wait for the staff to pick up. Others had begun leaving and now there were more empty tables than full. I was glad to go.

Anson followed me, although Deborah stayed seated with Nils, reluctant to go or perhaps hoping to make him see that she wasn't a monster for thinking so much about the murder at the rest stop.

Anson and I were alone in the elevator, heading to our floor. "I hate hotels," he confessed.

I smiled, a genuine smile, finding a kindred spirit. No doubt his hatred was different from mine, perhaps the zombie-like impersonality of them, or the smells or whatever, but I could understand his dislike.

"Me too."

Anson said nothing else and we road silently on the elevator the mirror above us minimizing the shadows that lingered in the corners behind us like silent partner on our ride as we listened to 1980s pop music gone instrumental.

I got off, not looking back, not wanting to spend too much time staring at the shadows. If I had been a target and the spirit had found a new one, why was it still after me? Why from so far away?

Now that it was night, the lights had been slightly dimmed in the hallway. It wasn't dark and it wasn't hard to see, but larger puddles of shadow fell from the walls. The carpet looked lest festive, an autumn evening rather than a summer afternoon. No doubt the softening of the light was some psychological thing that the hotel had learned of or perhaps it just used less energy and they were saving money.

I found my room and opened the door.

I had left the lights on. I looked around. I waited, my door open, standing halfway out in the hallway. Anson was well on his way to his room and would be unlikely to stand and stare, wondering why I didn't go right in.

I heard a television, probably the elephant person upstairs. I smiled and took a step in.

There were shadows around the room but not too many. I looked in the bathroom. It appeared safe enough.

I let the door latch behind me.

TRACI: SEPTEMBER NOW

I am a restless sleeper at best, and the hotel made things worse. The strange smells, mostly of cleansers brought to mind the Steely Woods Rest Stop and the last time I'd been there. Maybe I should have confronted my fears and gone back, but I'd never been able to make myself do it. The fact that another person had been killed there suggested that the haunting I had experienced there was real. I wasn't crazy.

Although, in my darkest moments, the worst of my nightmares, the ones that started with a single faucet drip followed by skeletal fingers, hard and cold against my head, those made me wish for insanity.

I heard every guest who got up to use the toilet and flushed. I heard a few people pass particularly bad gas. I heard the ping of the elevator throughout the night, my ears straining, even in sleep, to hear everything around me, and particularly for that stray faucet drip that came only once.

I was fortunate in that I did not hear it. I was careful when I'd washed up in the sink to make sure the faucet was tight and no water dripped. I did the same for the shower, which had had good water pressure and wonderful warmth that was almost enough to relax me, though I am never fully relaxed.

In the morning, I was the first up, my bag at my ankle, having a cup of hot water, not coffee, lest I be forced to use the communal bathroom in the studio too often. I ate a decent breakfast paid for by the bank and was finishing when Anson and Nils came down. Deborah arrived last, looking a little bit the worse for wear.

"All that salad," she said seating herself at our table and gesturing to the waitress for coffee. "It just ruined me. I don't know, maybe there was something in it. You know, salmonella or something. I don't know how I'll get through today."

From the way Anson grimaced as he ate his eggs, I knew he thought she could have kept some of that particular information to herself.

"I hope you'll be fine working," Nils said. "I believe I've decided between two of the voice actors and I'd like to get this wrapped up today."

Which meant we'd be leaving for Charlotte that night. I was thankful I'd not have to spend another night at the hotel. While pleasant enough, it wasn't home. I might not have as many neighbors in my condominium complex as I did in the hotel but I knew their routines, knew the common noises, and those rarely scared me.

Anson and Nils ate quickly while Deborah sipped her coffee. I finished my hot water. I had ascertained that the ladies room downstairs was a room with only a toilet and sink. I could use that. I wouldn't be hearing something from two stalls down, walking towards me, slowly gaining on me while I was trapped inside the stall with nowhere to go.

Anything to put off having to use a stall at the radio. I was good about holding it at work, though I'm sure doctors would be horrified. Nils had a private bath in his office and at lunch I could go in there, usually. Sandy was aware that I hated public bathrooms and she said nothing to me when I slipped in. Her kindness was probably the only thing that allowed me to keep working.

Ridiculous, I know, but that was the way the horror had wrapped itself around me, dug in its skeletal fingers, kept me from having a real life, a normal life.

The day went quickly. I had no reason to use the stalls in the studio because this time we went out to lunch, things moving along more quickly than expected. And small restaurants often have a single toilet. Those small favors let me get through the main part of the day without fear or raising my heart rate too much, except for the time a stray shadow seemed to follow me into the conference room, though there was no body to join it. But Anson sat in there, sketching, and the shadow melted away, shy in front of someone unknown.

On the car ride back, I sat in back with Anson again. Deborah claimed the front having been under the weather all day from her salad. I was beginning to wonder if there really had been something in it.

We left late enough that we hit only the tail end of rush hour in Raleigh. Between Charlotte and Raleigh we made good time, although Deborah had us stop at a gas station for a pit stop. And then we stopped at a rest area just off of I-85 outside of Salisbury.

Rest stops in the East are different from those in the west. Although it rains in Washington, most have several buildings joined by covered walkways. In the east, rest stops are usually buildings with a men's room on one side and women's room on the other. Some have a general information desk in the center and others are joined to a fast food restaurant.

Anson and Nils exited the car when Deborah hopped out, hurrying to the low cream colored brick building. Lights lit the walkway from the parking lot to the building, leaving few shadows on the steps. The parking lot was darker with large swaths of inky shadows between the safety circles of brightness from the tall lights that lit the lot.

I followed the others into the building. This one was one of the smaller rest areas, just a big lobby in white tile and two bathrooms along the back. Maps hung on one wall and the other had a row of windows. A group of benches had been placed in the middle. I'd have sat, but that would have required I turn my back to the bathroom doors and I had no desire to do so. Instead I leaned against the wall with the map.

My bladder added pressure, reminding me that I needed to go and Charlotte was still a fair ways away. But I couldn't.

Several trucks were parked in the darkened lot outside, but ours was the only car. While there were plenty of other cars rushing along the highway outside, they offered only the faintest white noise in the background. Deborah would be the only other person in the restroom with me, in a place where I wouldn't be able to see everything. There was no way I could go in there.

Anson and Nils came out and milled around. Deborah didn't reappear. I started to get antsy. I was in a place where others could relieve themselves and I badly wanted to, but I knew I couldn't go in. I tried to keep my fidgeting to a minimum.

"You think you should check on her?" Nils asked looking at me.

I didn't want to, but how could I explain that I'd nearly died in a rest area bathroom and was phobic about them?

I nodded. I didn't need to go into a stall and use it, placing myself in the vulnerable position of being caught, quite literally, with my pants down. I just had to go in and look for Deborah and find out what was taking her so long.

I slipped inside.

Tiny tiles that had once been white and were now cream and gray lined the floors. Larger tiles in the same cream lined the walls halfway up. Pale off-white paint covered the rest. In a corner someone had scribbled a name but it had faded or been partially washed off. Four sinks covered the wall on my right, with two hand dryers at the end. An empty paper towel dispenser hung next to them.

Eight stalls with beige dividers were on my left. I bent down. Only one pair of feet towards the end.

"Deborah?" I called. I didn't yell. I didn't whisper.

My voice sounded too loud in the room. It was like calling in an empty room, as if there were no feet beneath one of the doors.

One of the faucets dripped.

Just once.

I backed up towards the wall, my heart in my throat, burning and aching as if someone were pulling it up and out from my body.

I thought I heard a step on the floor.

I brought a hand to my face. I didn't want to look, but couldn't not look.

I should run. Tried to get my feet to move, but they wouldn't. I had no control. I was lucky urine wasn't streaming down my leg because my bladder suddenly felt it was about to burst and I had so little control of anything I didn't know why it wasn't happening.

I don't know how long I stood like that.

Long enough that Anson and Nils came looking for me.

"What's going on?" Anson asked.

"I see her feet, but she didn't answer," I said. "I thought I heard something but I couldn't see anything."

Nils gave me a long look. Probably taking in my shaking hands. No doubt my face was pale. I was shivering all over, chilled to the bone though it wasn't cold in the restroom. Rather it was comfortable.

"Deborah?" Anson called louder than me. If anyone were in the men's room they'd hear him.

No response.

"Second to the last stall," I said.

Nils looked under the door.

"Maybe you should open it?" he said. There was something pleading in his eyes but also sorrow. Like he knew I was terrified of what I'd find, but he had to make me do it. How would it look if a boss burst in on an employee when she was in a stall in the public restroom?

Braver now that I wasn't alone, I walked towards the stall. I paused to hit all of the others, opening doors, making sure they were all empty. Only Deborah's didn't open.

I didn't want to crawl down on the floor. Instead I went into the stall next to hers and climbed on the toilet. I kept my purse at an angle so the door couldn't close, locking me alone in the stall.

I reached my hand up, fingers curling over the top of the stall, not unaware that this was exactly what the creature had done at Steely Woods.

I stood up, imagining my head rising over the top, the brown hairs on my head visible first and then the roundness of my skull and the pale cream of my forehead, lighter than usual because of the harsh light and the terror I was still experiencing. I would look to Deborah not unlike the creature had looked to me that night in Steely Woods.

Deborah leaned against the far cubical divider, her head down. Red pooled from her lower body, a tiny bit of splatter had landed on her pants which were just above her knees, barely hanging on. One drop had landed on the floor to the side.

I screamed as I dropped off the toilet, throwing myself out of the stall.

"What?" Nils asked.

"911." I couldn't say anything else. I could hardly breathe. I needed air. I needed to get out of there. I rushed through the restroom and out to the main room, gasping. The lights were on, but I was alone. No one came in. I saw a trucker by his cab, smoking. Maybe talking on his cell phone. Nothing else.

I wanted to run out, run away, but darkness covered the parking area.

I heard a faucet drip, loudly, like I was in a bathroom. I whirled, letting out another gasp. My chest tightened further squeezing out every last bit of air. I needed to scream again and again but without air I could barely whisper. I was going to die.

Something banged and crashed. Swearing.

I pictured the creature coming after Nils and Anson, tearing them apart, leaving them for dead before coming out after me. I needed to leave.

Something screeched across the floor. Claws against tile.

Voices.

Coming closer.

I was pressed back against the wall, no longer even trying to breathe, as if by not breathing, I wouldn't be seen by anything, supernatural or otherwise. How could it have happened, so silently? How could Deborah not have heard something?

Nils came out of the bathroom with Anson. Nils was on the phone, telling someone where he was. Anson looked pale. His hands shook as he rushed out of the building, pausing near the entrance. I followed. I didn't want to be alone at the rest stop.

Not again.

TRACI: SEPTEMBER NOW

The wait for the police and the medics was interminable. I really needed to use the bathroom. Nils guided me into the men's room and stood watch at the door so someone else couldn't come in. Anson waited near the door of the women's room in order to turn anyone else away.

I finished what I needed to do quickly, leaving the stall door slightly ajar. If Nils noticed or if he thought that was odd, he said nothing. He'd probably think it had to do with Deborah.

I hurried out of the men's room barely noticing that it was a mirror image of the women's room. No faucets dripped. No odd sounds, although it smelled of ammonia and bleach so strongly that I even smelled it through my stuffed up nose. Or maybe I felt it rather than smelled it.

I hardly looked at my face, which was blotchy red and white, red from tear stains, white from pallor. It reminded me of the single red dot of blood that had landed on the tile floor in the other bathroom, the blood that had belonged to

Deborah. If I had been able to keep myself together, might she still have been alive?

Medics were arriving as I came out of the men's room. Anson directed them to the women's room and they hurried on in. A police officer followed and paused to talk to Anson.

The truck driver that I had seen smoking was looking over at the building. He was clearly talking to someone on a cell phone because when he moved into the light, I saw his lips moving.

Another police officer arrived. He spoke to Nils and me. I stood mute, not even sure what he was asking. Nils' words were equally unintelligible to me. I felt as if my brain had shut off any semblance of communication. I saw things. I knew things. I heard and felt things. I even smelled things a little bit but I couldn't process them with words. It was all sensation for me at the moment.

The police officer looked at me and said something before leaving. I probably looked blank.

The truck driver moved out of the light and started for his truck. Another man got out of the sleeper section of his cab and looked around. The man who had been on the phone started the truck, the loud low purr of sound. The squeaky hiss of air as the brakes came off.

I felt one of the police officers brush by me as he hurried outside to see who was leaving.

I wanted to tell him it didn't matter. I'd have seen a man, a human, coming out of the restroom. I had seen no one. There were no other exits. The bathroom had a single window, narrow and high, too small for a grown man to leave through.

I didn't say anything. My mouth couldn't move. I had thoughts, too many of them, but no words.

Everything was a blur and a haze and even the real people, the people around me, started to fade out.

The lobby darkened like someone had turned off the peripheral lights. I wanted to move, to find out who had turned off the lights, but I stood frozen. Voices became a low buzz and then faded out until I was alone with my thoughts and imaginings.

I was so tired.

I got cold, so cold.

It was hard to breathe.

"Are you going to tell them?" a voice said. A girl's voice, perhaps high school.

I didn't know what she meant.

"About me. And you? Or are you worried they'll think you're crazy?"

I had nothing to say to that. The voice was right. I *was* worried they'd think I was crazy.

"Maybe they'll even think you did it!" Laughter then, around me.

I tried to shake my head, clear it out.

"Let them catch the guy leaving. Who knows what else he's done," the voice said. "Don't say you didn't see anyone. Say you didn't think anyone had gone in there. They won't believe you anyway."

I wanted to ask who was speaking but my tongue stuck to my mouth.

I opened my eyes, realizing only then that I'd somehow sunk into a light sleep. A dream.

Police officers walked through the rest stop building, their steps purposeful. Nils sat next to me, Anson on his other side. They both looked as confused and horrified as I felt.

Nils looked at me, met my eyes. "I'm so sorry I insisted you go in there and find her," he said.

I shrugged. It didn't matter. What mattered was that Deborah was dead, murdered practically in front of us and we'd been able to do nothing. My stomach rolled. How did one stop a murderous spirit?

I'd thought about that now and again, but Deborah's murder suddenly brought the question close to home. I was certain that she—for some reason I knew the ghost was a she —had killed Deborah because of me. Maybe it was the dream, but maybe the dream wasn't exactly a dream.

Or maybe, I worried, I was just going crazy. I had seen ghosts, lived in fear, and now…

Now, I was hearing voices.

Nils shifted beside me but I didn't look. I didn't want to see the worry in his eyes, worry not for what had happened to Deborah, but for me and what had happened to me.

LUCY: SUMMER THEN

Alma pushed Lucy along through the woods. The sun was still up, but the sky was beginning to pink. Time no longer held meaning for Lucy, though she felt her body clench at the sun falling because so many of the men her sister insisted she allow to use her came with the failing light.

Alma didn't normally bring her to the woods, where the evergreens grew tall and the air smelled of life and death, the aroma of pine pitch and decaying vegetation. The birds fell silent as they passed noisily through the trees.

"Where?" Lucy asked. She'd stopped trying to engage her sister in any conversation. Anything she said had a snap to it that would cause Alma to slap her, or, in her anger, insist Lucy service even more men.

Lucy had taken to smoking Alma's cigarettes when she could get them. That annoyed her sister further because cigs were expensive, or so Alma said. Lucy hadn't ever purchased them. It had been over a month since she'd gone out, gone to the post office or gone anywhere even in town to see what was happening. She didn't want to be seen.

Alma either didn't notice or didn't care.

Lucy knew she was dying and her sister didn't care.

"Don't worry about it," Alma said. "You'll do what you always do when you get there. This guy likes it to be in his home."

Lucy didn't like that. Didn't like it one bit.

"You'll stay outside so I know how to get home?" she asked, her voice small like a child's.

Alma didn't answer or if she did the words were lost in the air.

Though it was summer and in the sun it was warm, beneath the trees it was cool, particularly when there was a breeze. Lucy shivered.

They passed behind the town. Lucy smelled old bacon and coffee from the café though the trees kept her from seeing it. She heard a dog bark and though she heard a car pass but that was so faint she couldn't be certain.

Alma hurried now.

Lucy's feet slowed, even as her sister tried to go faster. For her transgression, Lucy received another shove, one that nearly pushed her over.

"He doesn't want you to be late. He'll be angry if you're late and I don't want to think about what will happen then," Alma said.

Lucy shuddered. Alma was afraid of this man. Lucy was going to have to be with a man that frightened Alma. Nothing frightened her sister who was as resilient as they came. Lucy had no idea what kind of person would frighten her.

Her stomach knotted tighter than ever. It was always in a knot and she always felt as if she was just a breath away from vomiting. She didn't think she was pregnant because there always seemed to be blood. How could a child live through that?

Alma turned towards town and they had passed behind it, a spirit avoiding the eyes of the living. Their destination was just on the edge of town, where Lucy heard goats off in the distance and a chicken clucked.

The house they were going to was a narrow thing, built by hand and put together with wood from here and there giving it the look of an eyesore. It was bigger than the trailer, though, and Lucy noted the power lines that connected it to the world, something she and Alma didn't have. They had the generator salvaged and pampered and serviced by the men that Lucy in turn serviced. Before that, the generator had cost money.

Alma knocked on the door, painted in deep blue, unlike the browns and grays of the wood that lined the house. A window was next to the door but the light was wrong so Lucy couldn't see in.

A man with a beard came to the door. He filled the frame, his brown hair that curled up around his skull nearly touching the top. His beard was long and dark. The hands that held out the money, a thick pile of bills that Lucy saw were at least twentys, were filthy with grease. There was a line along one side of his neck as if he'd wiped sweat there and the grease had stayed.

Closer, Lucy smelled motor oil. The man wore brownish work pants. Lucy wasn't sure whether they were dirty or if they came that color. His short-sleeved shirt was a dull cream, creased and stained with gray splotches.

"That her?" the man asked.

Alma nodded.

"I'll be near town for when she can come home. She's not sure she knows the way," Alma said quietly, her head not meeting the man's eyes.

"It'll be awhile." His voice was low and grumbled like a bear in a cave.

Lucy tried to hold down her fear.

Alma backed up and pulled Lucy closer to the stoop that created a small entry to the house.

Lucy entered.

The place was dark. Inside the main room was paneled. There was a big radio on a table, made of wood, probably pine, that looked handmade. A sofa sat against the wall where the window was.

A door led into another room that Lucy thought was a kitchen. She heard the hum of a refrigerator.

A hall led off to the right.

The man led her to the one bedroom. Across the way, she saw the mismatched tile of a bathroom that held a toilet, a sink, and a shower. What luxury.

He undressed her and didn't speak as he ran his hands over her body, squeezing her breasts that were always tender from men's touch. His beard trailed down her skin, once so soft, and made it itch. Lucy pushed away tears, closing her eyes, pretending to be somewhere else, anywhere else but with this huge man.

When she thought he was nearly done, his hands wrapped around her neck and he began to squeeze.

Lucy thrashed, trying to pull them away. She couldn't breathe. He was going to kill her.

Her heart raced. She began to sweat.

The tears she had fought came to her eyes, making her angry because she didn't want to cry in front of him.

Then she got really angry because she was going to die before making Alma pay for what she'd done to her. Lucy wanted to scream and she thrashed harder, kicking the man in the side.

And with that, he laughed. A long low chuckled as if he were pleased.

The hands loosened from around her neck.

Lucy sucked in a breath.

"I love a fighter," he said.

Lucy gasped a few more times.

He pushed her out of the bed while she was still gasping, still trembling and told her to get dressed and get lost. He'd tell her sister when he wanted her again.

Lucy was left in no doubt that he'd want her again.

As she dressed she tried to hold onto her anger at Alma. It was safer than the terror she was living with.

13

TRACI: SEPTEMBER NOW

Somehow we made it back to Charlotte. Nils dropped me at my condo and told me not to worry about my car. I hadn't even thought about it in the bank employee garage. It was the last thing on my mind.

Nils hesitated as he dropped me home, as if he wondered if he should offer to see me to the door. I didn't say anything, still in shock. I had talked to police but didn't recall what I had said. I hoped I was coherent.

The parking lot of my complex was dark, lit only by lights that left too many shadows. Normally I tried to avoid it at night but it's not like I had a choice that night unless I wanted to remain in the van. The lights that might have shown from windows had long since been turned off. That long after midnight, only a few beacons guided me towards the building.

I hurried as best I could, encumbered by my suitcase. I would have left it the van but Nils reminded me of it. I scurried off like a rat scared by the sounds around him.

My hands shook as I tried to get my keycard to the outside of the building to work. It took me three tries.

Finally the door unlatched and I was welcomed into the minimally lit lobby. Bright enough for most people, but all I noted were the way the shadows puddled in the corners. The large desk, normally manned by a guard in the daytime sat silent and empty. At night, locked doors were considered sufficient.

I would have been glad of company, happy to pay more in dues to have someone waiting at the desk no matter the hour of the night. I didn't care that packages wouldn't come that late, leaving a watcher bored and perhaps sleepy.

I walked through the lobby, staying to the brightest areas. The white tile reflected what light there was, the gold veins creating a pleasant enough color. The brightness was one reason I had chosen the building. I by-passed my mailbox so shrouded in shadow.

I hurried to the elevator, dancing impatiently as it came down from the fifth floor. When it finally arrived, I rode up to the third floor. This elevator wasn't as brightly lit as the one in the hotel. Matt black floors greeted me and walls lined in a brown colored panel that usually looked caramel, but that night looked like melted chocolate in the dim light, were dark enough to make me cringe.

My floor was quiet. I heard someone snoring from the condo nearest the elevator. They must have been sleeping in the living room because the bedroom should have been too far away for someone to hear. Besides, the walls were well insulated and I was rarely annoyed by my neighbors. I hoped they felt the same way about me.

My condo was dark when I unlocked the door. I felt for the switch and flipped it on. I held my breath, worried for an instant that nothing would happen and the place would stay plunged in the darkness. But the light worked fine.

My refrigerator kicked out an ice cube. The place smelled

of basil and garlic from the spaghetti I had made before leaving.

I walked in, flicking on all the other lights. I dragged my suitcase behind me. I needed to get the electric lanterns out in case of a power failure. I was exhausted and shaky but I knew I wouldn't sleep until that chore had been taken care of.

Opening my bag I quickly found them and lit them, setting them around the apartment in their appropriate places. Tonight of all nights I needed the light.

I breathed out. I was home. I was as safe as I was going to get. I sat down on the bed and removed my socks.

In my bathroom, a faucet dripped.

Once.

I whimpered.

Tears fell from my eyes. There was only so much terror I could take.

I wanted to start screaming, but didn't know who would come. My fellow condo dwellers would probably think someone had their television on too loudly. By the time the police arrived, I'd be dead.

The lights stayed on, bright.

One of my electric lamps started to buzz a little.

I picked one up and took it with me to the hallway.

I edged a foot into the hall feeling the wall press against my back.

My eyes were open, though tears still streamed from them.

My heart pounded so loudly that if the faucet dripped again, I wouldn't hear it.

My body smelled too sweet, sickly, as if I'd just had a fever and it had only recently broken.

I drew in a breath, too short. Not enough air for me, but I

couldn't breathe in any deeper, feeling as if a boney arm were crushing my throat.

I edged my foot further along the hallway, feeling the cool laminate flooring beneath my toes. My feet were icy from the internal chill and then the coolness of the floor. Normally I liked the feel of it, reminding me that I was in a safe building.

I craned my neck to look around the bathroom door.

I saw nothing.

I slipped my foot in a little further and looked again.

The bathroom was empty.

There was the faintest shadow in the shower but that could have come from the angle of the shower curtain.

I breathed out, watching.

I stood there longer than I should have as the clocked ticked later into the night, until enough time had passed that it was no longer late, but early.

At some point my eyes started to close and I slipped back to my bedroom.

Nothing had been there. Or so I hoped.

I undressed quickly and pulled on sweats. I curled up in my covers and attempted to sleep.

Sometime in the early morning hours, my upstairs neighbors started moving around, making their normal morning sounds. I dropped off.

And dreamed.

I was back at Steely Woods Rest stop. The branches of the trees were bare in the fall night, reaching towards me like skeletal arms ready to grab. The lights of the buildings, all disconnected cream brick joined only by covered walkways, looked like the eyes of a jack-o-lantern. The main building where coffee and cookies were served became a dark maw.

I didn't want to be there, not again.

A breeze blew, rattling the boney trees. The rush of traffic whizzed by on the interstate. I was already scared.

I stared at the building where I'd nearly died, waiting for something to happen. I had no idea what I expected to happen, but I waited there.

"Who are you?" I whispered.

Laughter met me. It grew louder until my ears filled with buzzing.

I opened my eyes, back in my bed. Terror overcame me when I realized the sound was still there, filling the room. It took me a moment but to realize it was only the alarm on my phone. I hadn't turned it off the night before.

Nils had said I didn't need to come in.

I was still exhausted. I wouldn't be able to work but I couldn't imagine sitting around the condo listening for the single drip of a faucet.

It was my fault Deborah was dead. I needed to set something right. I'd run that night at Steely Woods, too terrified to continue. I'd gotten lucky. Two teenagers had come into the building just as the creature was about to murder to me in the stall. When they arrived it disappeared.

Someone else had died that night, but I didn't hear about it until I got home.

And now another woman had died there. And Deborah, so fascinated with the deaths, had died here.

I was the link. The only link.

This had to be my fault.

I'd gotten away, not because I was smarter or because I was more fearless than anyone else, but because I'd gotten lucky.

I'd been closer to Deborah when she died, so very close. I could have died with her, easily. My luck had held, but only just.

14

TRACI: SEPTEMBER NOW

I spent the day dozing and then working on the computer. I had a laptop that I normally used on the kitchen table. Today, however, I curled up with it in my bed, pillows tucked behind me.

Sunlight came through the large window at my side. I had no music playing so I could listen for sounds that didn't belong.

My ears strained to hear anything, and as a result, I heard the murmurings of phone calls from the man next door and a conversation from the my neighbor on the fourth floor.

I knew when the air conditioner was kicking in and I noticed when it went silent.

Smells didn't seem to relate to my experience, though I recalled the smells of dirty diaper and bleach.

I searched through the internet, looking for deaths at rest stops. There were more than I expected. I had no idea if all the people were actually killed at rest stops but they seemed to be a prime place for hiding bodies. I should have given up my search after multiple articles about creepy deaths at rest stops and unsolved murders. Still, I hoped to find something out about Steely Woods.

The woman, Renee Parsons of Olympia Washington who had died in my place was mentioned on several of the sites. The latest victim, Alice O'Dell, showed up in a couple of news stories.

I looked up murders at rest stops and the same general articles repeated. I searched more specifically for murders at Steely Woods and came up with the information Anson and Deborah had imparted about the fact that every nineteen years or so someone seemed to die there. It had begun in 1970. I searched further and found that the first rest stops in that area were built around 1954, which would have been after 1951. Did that mean that the first person to die had died there in 1954? I bit my lip, wondering about it.

I did some more sleuthing to find which cities and towns were closest to Steely Woods. There were some small communities and I searched for murders there. There was a girl found in 1951 not far from the highway, before there was a rest stop. I didn't find anything for anyone earlier.

I made a few notes.

As the afternoon went on, although I was still feeling like I was in shock over Deborah, I realized I was less frightened than I'd been in years. I should have been terrified, having gone over the details of what I remembered so many times, but I wasn't. I felt like I was doing something. I felt strong.

Despite feeling strong, I jumped when the phone rang while I was working.

I looked at the number. Nils.

"Hey Nils," I said, picking up.

"Are you okay?" he asked. No preamble, nothing.

"I'm getting there," I said. "I think I still don't believe it happened. I think about going into work tomorrow and I expect that I'll see Deborah there."

"You don't need to come in right away. Don't even think about using sick time either. We were on a work excursion when this happened. I sent you in there to find her. When I think of how you could have been murdered as well…" Nils trailed off. "I'll make sure any time you take isn't taken off your sick time."

I had a feeling Human Resources wouldn't be pleased to hear the way Nils was talking. Likely he was also still in a state of shock. I wondered how Anson was.

"Are you at the office?" I asked.

He said he was. He talked about telling everyone and the reactions. All of this was processed carefully.

"We're worried about you," he said finally.

"It was a shock to find her," I said. "I think I'm recovering now."

Nils made a few sounds, so solicitous.

"How is Anson?" I asked.

"Oh he came in," Nils said. "He's busy doing some graphics. Said it would help not to be alone. I know I said you didn't have to come in, but I was worried about you. Being alone, I mean."

"I didn't really sleep. I dropped off about the time I'd be getting up. I considered coming in late but didn't know that I'd be able to focus."

Nils made some conciliatory remarks and reminded me that I could take more time.

I wondered how bad I'd been the day before, what I might have said that had gotten him so concerned. What would he think when I came in the next day and was ready to go? I was a new woman. I was ready to confront my ghosts.

I hung up the phone and the faucet in the bathroom dripped.

Once.

I started to cry.

Not just out of fear but out of anger at the fear that I was still feeling.

I pulled the covers up to my chin and tried to figure out if I'd be better off getting up and checking or hiding in the bedroom.

I stayed that way for longer than I should have. Long enough for me to realize that the sense of power I had gotten from believing I was doing something had been an illusion. I was not ready to confront my ghost and I wouldn't be until I understood what it was that I was confronting and how I could save myself.

If I could save myself.

TRACI: SEPTEMBER NOW

I went back to work the next day. I didn't expect to get a lot done, but like Nils and Anson, I wanted to be there. I didn't want to be home focusing on Deborah's death. My condominium, which had always seemed so safe, with its hardwood that shone in the light, pushing back shadows, and it's bright shiny tiles in the kitchen and bathroom that allowed me to see in all corners, keeping darkness at bay, no longer seemed so bright and safe no matter how many lights I turned on and how many electric lanterns I placed around.

My faucet washers that had been tightened to within an inch of their lives and been replaced at the first sign of a drip had begun to drip just once every few hours. There was a chill in the condominium that had nothing to do with the air conditioning. In fact, there were moments when I felt a cold breeze, a slight touch at the back of my neck, and the air wasn't on at all.

I had to get out. To be with people.

I took my personal laptop with me to work, taking the Lynx, the local light rail that ran only half a mile from my home and stopped just a few blocks from the bank. At one time I had looked into taking it regularly but I had forgotten about it when I'd had to leave late one evening in the winter. The lights hadn't been very bright and more shadows than people had crowded the cars.

That morning, like most mornings, there were plenty of people crowding around me, keeping me safe with their bodies, their warmth, their aliveness. Perhaps that very aliveness was a light to drive away the ghosts and if I stayed surrounded by people all the time, I'd not have to fear. Then again, Deborah had been alive once, too.

My office felt cold, and I immediately wished I worn a sweater over my long sleeved pullover and blue knit skirt. I probably could have arrived in jeans, but I didn't want to push it. It was enough that I expected to get only minimal amounts done, perhaps some routine work on the computer.

Although sun came in through the glass, hitting my chair, I continued to be cold as I worked. My fingers felt stiff from the chill that ate away at my flesh and creeped into my bones.

Will came in and talked with me, asking me how I was. I gave him my general answer. He looked at me sadly, not quite meeting my eyes, but closer than usual.

Anson came in not long after. He glanced around the office and rubbed his arms, as if he, too, felt the chill.

"I couldn't believe what happened," he said, "and I can't believe we made you see that."

"You saw her too." I wasn't sure why he and Nils were so protective.

"You just looked so terrified of having look into the stall. It was like you had a premonition or something." Anson picked at the arm of the chair he sat in. The bright blue cloth was smooth but he was making it even smoother as he talked.

"Maybe I did." Perhaps I could just be considered psychic instead of crazy and fearful, which was probably a more accurate description. "I mean, I didn't know what I'd see, but when Deborah didn't answer and she was clearly there, I had a feeling something terrible had happened. I guess I just expected to be wrong." The last was a lie. I had expected to find her dead. I had been more surprised that there wasn't a pool of blood and spatter all over, like a scene from a horror movie. Deborah's death had been almost too clean and tidy.

Anson nodded. "I have to say, you were pretty out of it after. I can't say I blame you. I think I was too. Everything I did was on autopilot. I got nothing done yesterday. I worked on graphics and tossed everything. I just can't get in the groove and I know we need that stuff soon."

"Did Nils give you the talk about how we aren't supposed to push ourselves?" Maybe Nils was only talking to me, perhaps expecting Anson to feel normal after all of this.

"I got it. I can even take some time off. I guess Nils is looking into what it takes for a compassionate leave thing. Normally it's so that someone who has a death in the family doesn't have to use all their vacation and sick time, but Nils thinks this qualifies."

So perhaps Nils wasn't overpromising and HR wouldn't be on his case if Anson and I took some time off. I considered what I'd do with it.

"It's so weird," Anson went on, "we were all talking about the death at the rest stop in Washington and then this happened."

"It is weird," I said. "And it's weird that the deaths happened more than once at Steely Woods. I looked up that information yesterday, you know."

Anson looked up, eyes wide. I must have made it very clear I wasn't interested.

"I mean, suddenly we were involved." Maybe I had always been involved. I just hadn't realized how. "I didn't find multiple deaths at any others. I think maybe one other rest area had a couple of deaths, but they seemed more random than Steely Woods."

Anson nodded. "Do you think there's a connection? Like because Deborah had lived in both places? Maybe someone was stalking her? But you didn't see anyone else there, did you?"

I shook my head. I hadn't seen anyone. I didn't dare tell Anson I was thinking about a creature. I was still afraid. Afraid of being labeled as crazy. Afraid of realizing I really was crazy. I was also afraid that the ghost or creature or whatever it was had found me and was toying with me.

"I just don't understand how someone could have come in and out without you seeing them." Anson wasn't going to let that go.

"Maybe I closed my eyes for a few minutes," I said. "And maybe dozed just enough to miss them? It was lucky if they walked out just then."

Anson looked away. "It feels coincidental."

"Then what are you saying?" I asked.

"Well, you were the only one out there. And you didn't see anyone going in or out…"

"So you're saying *I* did it?" My voice raised higher. I was both terrified of the idea of being accused and angry that he'd say something like that. But perhaps that was the ghost's plan after all. I was too guarded to be killed, but if she could make it look like I had murdered someone that would be punishment as well. Besides, in prison I wouldn't be in control of lights or environment.

Anson was already shaking his head. "There wasn't that much blood, but you had none on you. There's no way. You were wearing the same clothing and brought only your handbag with you."

"Then what?" I asked.

"Maybe there was something weird about it. Maybe

there's a secret entrance through the back? Maybe it started as a service entrance and got changed. Or maybe there's a basement that we don't know about. Or maybe…"

I waited for Anson to finish what he was saying.

He didn't.

"You know that all of those are about as likely as me killing her? Or the trucker who I saw talking on the phone and who left when the cops showed up." I hated to suggest such a thing, but Anson couldn't walk down that path. He'd never let go of it.

Anson wouldn't let it rest. "Deborah is dead. Something happened to her in there. Nils and I didn't hear anything in the men's room and we weren't in there that long. If we'd gone in as soon we finished and found you waiting, we probably would have caught whoever, or whatever, killed her."

If she was killed by a ghost, would he have seen something? It was an interesting question. The ghost had disappeared when I was in the rest stop and the other girls had come in. If he'd gone in and the ghost was terrifying Deborah into silence then he'd have seen nothing and she'd have left, probably shaking. Knowing Deborah, surrounded by those of us she knew, she'd have talked about the experience, talked about thinking she was going to die.

Out in the lobby I hadn't heard a faucet drip. Not until I went into the bathroom. Had the men heard it out there? Had it happened for Deborah?

"I know it sounds crazy." Anson wouldn't look at me. "You probably think I am crazy and I deserve that, I'm sure, but I can't wrap my head around what happened."

"I don't think you're crazy," I said. "I hated talking to you and Deborah about what happened at Steely Woods because I had an incident happen to me there, too. It terrified me. I think the only reason I'm alive is because two teenagers happened along with their mother late at night and stopped whatever was going to happen. It's why I always use Nils' private bathroom and why I was so scared about going in after Deborah. Public restrooms with stalls remind me of what happened… and I'm still scared."

Anson was now looking at me with interest.

"What happened?" he asked.

"I don't know," I said. "It's hard to remember exactly what. But I do recall that I was terrified and that I was certain I was going to die. I have no idea what happened to Deborah or if it was connected to Steely Woods or if that guy I noticed on the phone did somehow get in there and do something to her, but I know what it's like to think you're crazy."

Anson looked around the office for a long time, his eyes taking in the view outside, the sunshine and the tall cream colored building that faced ours. He looked at the floor and the pattern on the carpet. Then he looked back down at the arms of the chairs, at the walls, at my brag wall with my diploma and awards.

Finally, he looked back at me. "Do you think you're the connection?"

I sighed. "I hope not. But what if I am?"

My stomach knotted and I grabbed the edge of my desk, just a little, trying to keep my hands from shaking. What had I done? Would Anson go to Nils and tell him I was a mental case?

Instead he just nodded carefully. "I don't know. But at least that makes some sense to me, you know? In a weird way. Because it's not that there's some random killer practically flying around the country murdering people in rest areas. It's like it gives it a pattern and I can understand that."

I breathed out, suddenly aware that I'd been holding my breath.

"Thank you for not thinking I'm crazy."

"If you're crazy, then I probably am too," Anson said. "And

maybe we are, but at least we can say it helps make sense of two killings on opposite sides of the country so close together. And if we aren't crazy…maybe it gives us a place to start to try and figure out why."

I smiled. Anson was so young, like I was once. And he hadn't faced what I had. But he was willing to work with me. To help me. Maybe I *could* do this. I just needed to figure out how.

TRACI: SEPTEMBER NOW

At some point I had to leave work and go home. It helped that Anson seemed to believe that there was a link between Deborah's death and the murder at Steely Woods. It was a silly thing, really, because I knew he couldn't actually help me. Even so, it felt good to have someone who believed me. It also gave me an excuse for thinking I was the link. After all, as Anson said, it made sense for our minds to try and find some connection with two senseless murders in such a short time, even if they were thousands of miles apart.

I hadn't told him I was studying the issue. I needed to learn about ghosts and ghost hunting. I hated the way that sounded, as if I expected to enroll in a university class and then have it all be over. Were such a thing possible, I'd have my life back by now.

While it stays pretty bright in September, I had to admit that my home felt dark. I had all the lights on and afternoon sun still streamed all gold and pink through the windows, but too many shadows lurked in the corners and the overhead lights appeared dull rather than bright. I had my air conditioning off, which made the place quieter than normal, but I still felt cold. If the chill hadn't come and gone from moment to moment, I'd have turned on the heat. Even so, I was tempted to do so.

The neighbors, at least, were normal. I heard the usual periodic flush of a toilet and the woman upstairs walking across the floor. I'd hear an additional heavier tread later in the evening when her husband or boyfriend was home. I smelled them having pizza. I had brought in a deli sandwich and cup of soup. It didn't smell nearly as much, but it would be warm and filling and allow me to work at my dining room table while the sun lasted.

I googled through a hundred different links about getting rid of ghosts. Ideas ranged from smudging with sage to protecting the entryways with garlic or salt. Given my love of Italian food, I had a feeling garlic wasn't going to work. An Asian ritual used orange peels and water. I bit my lip thinking how all of these rituals cleansed a place. My apartment wasn't haunted, I was.

The ghost had noticed me at Steely Woods and if a place needed cleansing, the rest stop was it.

Though my eyes tired and my brain tried to process all this new information, I kept reading. Ghosts usually had a reason for sticking around. If I could find out why the ghost did what she did, I might be able to stop her. The ritual of every nineteen to twenty years was interesting. Maybe that was how long it took her to have the power to kill, but I had a feeling the timing was more important than that.

I kept reading while the sun went down and my condo darkened despite the lights. I had my electric lanterns set so that they minimized shadows. Mostly, my home felt safe, but tonight, as last night, I sensed something had changed. I hadn't moved anything. The lights still worked. I'd gotten several new batteries for the lanterns, which, given the size of them, weren't cheap, and still shadows lounged in the corners, seeming too long and large to be normal.

I sighed. The kitchen sink dripped once. It echoed differently than the drip in the bathroom and that resonance didn't terrify me as much as the one in the bathroom did. I breathed in and out, feeling proud of myself for an instant.

The bathroom faucet dripped. Suddenly sweat broke out over my palms and I turned to stare down the hallway.

The hallway light flickered, once, then twice, threatening to leave the corridor in full dark. I held my breath waiting, noticing then that the other lights in the condo began to flicker, some going out all together for seconds at a time.

My heart began to pound and my breath came shorter. I wanted to stand, to flee the place, but my legs shook so badly I couldn't even begin to stand. I felt a breath of cold against my back.

I turned my head, so very slowly, knowing I would see nothing.

I turned back to the hallway, but nothing had moved. Even the lights had stopped their flickering.

I tried to calm myself again. I breathed in and out, the way one of the therapists had suggested. She'd actually suggested I close my eyes and do it, but I knew there was no way I'd calm down if I had my eyes closed.

I counted my breaths, breathing in for a count of three and breathing out for a count of three. The band of fear no longer pressed against my chest. My heart still pounded too fast and too hard, though.

I stayed alert for any other sounds, any other sensations, but nothing happened though I sat there until I heard the husband upstairs walking towards their bedroom. I drew in another breath and pushed myself up from the computer. I wouldn't work there any longer. It was getting late and I ought to pretend to be on a schedule for work.

I hoped to be clear enough at work tomorrow that I could get something done. I'd cleared my emails for the day, today, though it had taken me four times as long leaving me no time to consider any other projects. My mind remained too focused on Deborah's death and the connection it might have to Steely Woods.

Anson was right to question the timing of Deborah's death. I should have heard something. At the very least, Deborah should have moved a little bit, perhaps gasped, but I'd heard nothing. I didn't understand how someone could die so quietly.

If the ghost did it, the doors and walls wouldn't really offer protection, though I recalled the skeletal fingers holding the top of my door, a head about to peer over it and into the stall where I was, as if it couldn't just slip through them like Casper in an old cartoon.

I made a mental note about that. Could the ghost just come through walls or did it have to disappear and reappear in another place? Did that take some sort of concentration on the part of the apparition?

I still didn't know enough about ghosts. No matter how much I read, my answers weren't there. Information on ghosts was all guesswork and supposition. I'd picked up any number of books on hauntings, becoming known to the librarians around Portland after I'd first been attacked. It's why I moved across the country, putting as much running water between me and the rest stop ghost as I could, but there'd been no real answers and I hadn't had the heart to keep searching.

I may have lived in terror, but I'd assured myself I was safe. I existed in a state of fear, eschewing a normal life in order to remain safe from something I didn't understand. Deborah hadn't known about me, but she'd been fascinated by the deaths, thinking there was some story there. She'd wanted me to tell her what I knew, if anything. I'd failed her. Maybe if I'd talked to her, she'd have been warned or been able to call out when she'd been trapped in that bathroom.

If she had called out and I'd gone in, would I have seen the creature? Would we both have died? Could the two of us have made enough noise to bring Anson and Nils running to help, and perhaps turn the tide in favor of the living rather than the dead?

I suspected I'd not have been able to scream even with someone else there, but perhaps my presence would have given Deborah the ability to do so. Too many if onlys. I'd gone through even more if onlys when I'd first escaped and heard about another death there. I couldn't let regret paralyze me any more than fear.

I had to move forward. Even if it was just a baby step.

Telling Anson had been a baby step. I could keep going.

17

LUCY: SUMMER THEN

The sun set earlier and earlier and soon enough fall would completely settle into the Pacific Northwest. Lucy had thought it was there already but then suddenly the weather turned brilliant with sunny skies and days warm enough to go without a coat. A few leaves were beginning to fall although the true autumn colors hadn't begun for those trees and bushes that weren't evergreen.

Lucy had expected to start back to school, but Alma had told her not to go.

"Isn't it required?" Lucy asked.

Alma gave her a long look and shook her head. "Like the law looks after people like us."

"But I need to learn. How will I ever get out of here if I don't learn something?" Lucy missed her books, missed reading in the library because she didn't have a card. She'd not dared to go anywhere since Alma had begun using her.

Lucy dreaded the days she went out to the cabin most of all. The bearded man still wrapped his large hands around her neck long enough and hard enough to leave bruises.

Those allowed Alma to charge him even more, which, while it terrified Lucy, it pleased her sister.

Some nights Alma slept elsewhere. Lucy wondered where, but Alma had just waved her hand and said Lucy shouldn't worry about it. It wasn't so much that Lucy was worried. Instead, she was terrified and angry that Alma would leave her there in the run down trailer while Alma spent the money Lucy was earning for them.

"People like us don't ever get out of here," Alma said. "We just keep doing what needs to be done to put food on the table."

"I'd get an after school job," Lucy said. "If I had a degree, I might even do secretarial work and that would feed us even better."

Alma shook her head. "And what do we do until then? If you go to school looking like you do when you come home sometimes, people will start wondering what you're up to. And believe me, taking money for sex ain't legal. You want to end up in jail?"

"I'm not the one taking money," Lucy argued. Maybe she should make the men give her money, put some in her hands so that Alma wouldn't get it all. She could put a few dollars away and go somewhere else, somewhere no one knew her. She could walk as far as she could and camp out. They had stuff to do that.

A few months ago, she wouldn't have considered walking through the woods along the highway until she got to a town. Now it seemed like a decent idea.

"Don't you go splitting hairs. Lawyers love that and then we'd both be put in jail," Alma said. "I have a reputation to protect."

Lucy laughed.

Alma glared at her. "You better be here when I get home.

If I find out you've been going to school when I specifically told you not to, you'll be very sorry."

Lucy glared, wondering what her sister thought could be worse than what she'd already done to her. She looked down at the table. "Why didn't you just leave me when dad died?"

"Figured someone needed to look out for you. Foster homes are bad. Who knew you were such a selfish thing always wanting and wanting?" Alma didn't say anything else but turned to leave.

Lucy thought that was wrong. She wasn't the one always wanting. It was Alma. Maybe she'd always wanted but somewhere along the lines it had gotten too much for her to take care of her sister and now they were in this mess. Lucy wasn't sure what to do about it. Wasn't sure what she could do about it.

She finished the toast she'd made and then cleaned the table. She picked up another slice of bread and made a half of a sandwich with some left over chicken meat they had. She packed it carefully in an old sack and set off for school.

Alma couldn't stop her from learning. Maybe at school she could trace a map and find out where to head and who to talk to. She could talk to one of the school counselors about jobs. They all knew she and Alma were poor. Maybe there was something in town, something besides letting men pay Alma to use her body.

It was a long walk to the road and it was late so the bus had already gone. Lucy wasn't going to get to the school any time soon. It didn't matter, probably. She could talk to people. She'd already missed a day because Alma had kept her so busy the day before. She smiled, thinking about the teachers she liked and what subjects she might learn.

18

TRACI SEPTEMBER NOW

I didn't get much done on Friday, either. Nils passed along the tidbits of information Deborah's family had given him about funeral arrangements. They were having the service back in Washington for themselves and friends who lived in the area. The coroner hadn't released the body yet and no one knew when that would happen. The family suggested Nils contact a personal friend of Deborah's, one who lived in Charlotte. Perhaps a small ceremony could be done for her friends and coworkers here.

Nils passed that information onto Sandy who would be in charge of contacting the friend and helping organize a service.

Anson and I had few chances to talk as he was busy finishing some designs for print ads to go with the new radio spots. He needed to get them in. Nils might not be pushing us, but upper management would start to push if our department didn't keep up with our schedule. Money still needed to be made and the business still needed to grow.

When the day was finally over, I headed home promptly at five so no one could fault me for leaving early.

The sun still shone bright in the sky, although it hung lower than it had a month or so ago. Fall was coming and when it arrived, by the time I got to the condo, it would be dusk. I wondered if I would feel better moving further south, like maybe Florida where the sun would stay higher and brighter all year long.

Except now, I didn't really need that. I was going to confront my fears. After, it wouldn't matter if I lived in Alaska where I had to spend half the year with only a few hours of sunlight in a day.

I almost smiled at myself as I opened the door to my condominium. It was a rare thing for me and I was pleased about that. Who would know that having to plan how to take care of a ghost would bring me such joy?

I heated some soup on the stove and then settled in on the dining room table with my laptop. Although I often liked the ability to look out the window, I closed the blinds so the sun didn't hit the screen, and I sat facing the hallway. Just in case.

I had all the lights on even that early. I didn't care about using too much energy.

Friday night with my computer was probably not what I had dreamed for myself at nearly forty-five. I think I had dreamed of having children and a husband and perhaps having an early evening in or waiting up for the kids, depending upon when they'd been born. Instead I had hardly any friends simply because I rarely went out. Even on Facebook, I was only connected to those who had known me when I went to school and people from work, leaving me with few contacts by the standards of most social media users.

I sipped soup from a large mug. I could have made a sandwich but I wasn't particularly hungry. Even the nice aroma of the tomato basil didn't make me long for my usual grilled cheese. When it was gone, I rinsed the cup and set it aside.

I went back to the computer, reading carefully, following the threads that I managed to unravel about hunting down what ghosts wanted, as well as piecing together the history of Steely Woods Rest stop.

It was easy enough to find information about rest stops in general. There were a number of websites that detailed the history of them. Finding out about the building of one was harder. Finally, I found something from a page on the history of the county where Steely Woods was located.

There was a small population center about two miles from the freeway. It had once been a growing community, but with the influx of the interstate highway, people bypassed that little place because of the ease of travel north and south. The town didn't die, really. It sort of faded away until it was more of a rural location for those who didn't want to be too close to any town at all.

Once upon a time there had been a newspaper, and someone had helpfully scanned two decades worth of papers. While that seemed like a lot of work, the paper was only weekly, just two single legal sized sheets of a paper with a full third of it devoted to advertising.

From the newspaper, I found out that a young girl named Lucy Martin disappeared in the early autumn about eighty years ago. It appeared as if no one missed her for some time, so it was certainly possible she'd disappeared in September.

The school librarian had suggested that something happened to her and asked the police to investigate the sister. Nothing was proven. I searched for more information about Lucy but nothing came up. I did see her sister, Alma mentioned a few times in the paper. She was charged with solicitation once and another time she was charged with solicitation and fraud. Because of the fraud charge, she served time in jail.

I wondered what had happened to her after that but though I scanned the papers for some time after that, I didn't find another mention of her. Given that the papers were just scanned pages, I could find no way to do a better search.

I had a feeling I had a name.

"Isn't that right Lucy?" I whispered to myself. The apartment felt too quiet. I didn't even hear the woman upstairs moving around.

I glanced towards the window, the sheer blinds letting in light from the parking lot but not allowing me to make out any cars in the lot. While it was dark, it wasn't late enough for the complex to be that quiet.

I felt cold all of a sudden.

Then the faucet in the bathroom dripped. Once.

Chills ran up my arms.

While I still felt terrified, I gloried in the fact that I was certain I was onto something. Maybe Lucy even wanted me to continue.

"Did you know," I whispered, because speaking out loud seemed to echo in the apartment as if it were empty of everything, not just other humans, "that your sister Alma was arrested and went to jail for fraud and solicitation a few years after you disappeared?"

I waited. No faucet dripped. No chill came around.

Maybe I was just insane and reading things into random events. Maybe Anson was right and the whole concept of ghosts was just my brain's way of trying to make sense of a particularly unusual experience.

I drew in a breath, trying to figure out what I thought about that. Tears welled at the corners of my eyes. What if I really was just crazy? Maybe I hadn't seen anything in the rest stop and I was a crazy woman who had been living in fear that I shouldn't have had all these years. Maybe I should have said more to more of the therapists I'd visited. Maybe I'd have medications that would keep me from seeing those things.

I closed my eyes for a second, trying to hold back more tears and perhaps sobs. The fear, the knowledge that I knew deep down that I wasn't insane, that I had seen a ghost or some sort of supernatural creature and it had been trying to kill me had made up the warp and weft of my life all these years. To think that it was all a dark fantasy was too much.

I turned off the computer and decided it was close enough to bed time to retire. I'd change clothes and then sleep. I wondered if I'd sleep easier if I could convince myself I was just insane.

I walked down the hallway. I passed the bathroom, its door wide open and all the lights on. I even had an extra electric lantern there to drive out any unwanted shadows. I turned forward to look into my bedroom.

The lights flickered and died.

Even the electric lights.

I felt a cool brush against the back of my neck.

And then it was gone.

The electric lanterns came on again. The lights stayed off.

I turned around, hurrying back past the bathroom. I didn't want to be trapped in my bedroom if something happened. A lantern sat on the dining room table leaving a small circle of yellow light.

I got to my tiny dining area and breathed a sigh of relief. I peered out of the blinds but it was dark. Completely dark. No streetlights leaving puddles of yellow light around the cars in the narrow visitor's lot, no lights in the buildings across the way. The power was out. The actual power.

"If that was you and you're sending me a message," I said out loud, no longer whispering. My voice wasn't echoey any longer. "Then could you turn the lights back on? This freaks me out."

I waited.

Nothing.

Everything stayed dark.

I sighed, allowing thoughts of just being crazy, of manipulating facts to come to the fore once again. Before I could sink into the despair of one learning of one's inability to tell fantasy from fact, the lights flickered back on again.

I shuddered. Relieved to know I wasn't crazy. Terrified that I hadn't left behind the murderous ghost in Steely Woods nineteen years ago.

19

TRACI: SEPTEMBER NOW

I had all day Saturday to research. I decided to go out for coffee at the Starbucks just a short walk from my complex. It was early, not even nine, when I went, but cars were out, gliding along the roads just a little faster than they should have. A white Nissan Altima turned right from the left turn lane, not wanting to bother with going around the block.

I crossed at the light. Other people might risk running across several lanes of traffic, but I wasn't planning on taking chances. While the sun shone in the morning, I noted clouds in the distance which might mean a storm later in the day. I didn't worry about it. Even if I wanted to leave about the time it started raining, I'd learned that in Charlotte rain showers rarely lasted very long.

As I walked, I picked out the smells of coffee and car exhaust swirling around me. I hurried onward, listening to the low purr of cars. Passing a small deli, I heard music, something fast paced with drums. It didn't feel like morning music unless you'd been up all night and needed the kick. I wondered if the person playing it had already gotten his hit of caffeine from the Starbucks two doors down.

Opening the door, I noted two people in line, and a few others sitting around with drinks. One person waited on a drink near the counter, looking at a cell phone. A man in jeans and a plain gray t-shirt sat at a table in the corner with a computer and his fingers were flying over the keyboard. I wondered what he was writing.

The short line moved quickly. My coffee was a bit hotter than I liked but I had things to research and time to let it cool down. While the Starbucks lighting wasn't my ideal, there were plenty of people around. If I needed a bathroom break, their bathrooms were singles, which meant no stalls.

I wrapped my hands around my warm drink for a moment. I wasn't cold, exactly, but inside I felt chilled. Going out, even surrounded by people, and staying some place if I didn't have to was not normal for me.

I sometimes walked into the Starbucks and left again, on particularly sunny days, but I didn't know that I'd ever pulled up a chair and sat down to work. I chose the spot closest to the window which faced southeast so I had maximum sun. While it might be dim around me, I was in a puddle of sunlight.

While I knew the coffee hadn't had time to cool, it tempted me. I'd slept poorly after my encounter with Lucy and my body craved the caffeine. I moved the cup aside and started searching the internet for Lucy Martin, who disappeared eighty years ago in Southwest Washington. I doubted I'd find much. The name was common enough and I knew little other information.

I did search on Alma Martin, hoping the name was a little less common. Even then, I found far too many recent results, particularly links to social media. I tried to limit the searches to certain years but that didn't help. I limited it to Washington and while I got a lot of hits that weren't her, I did get a one that was clearly about her. An obituary. From Olympia.

It had to be her. I read carefully, hoping for any clue about her sister Lucy but found nothing.

Reading between the lines, it appeared that Alma wasn't particularly well liked. Her time in prison wasn't mentioned, merely hardships that had come her way until she met Lee Tucker who married her after a long courtship. She'd been a step-mother to his youngest son and she had no family of her own, having once had a sister who had run off and disappeared years before. Alma died at seventy-eight years old.

Old enough that the internet was around and her obituary was there, which was good for me. Old enough that I didn't think Lucy would appreciate how long her sister got to live. I did some calculations based on her age. Lucy had disappeared in 1942. Alma would have been nineteen. I wondered if Alma had murdered her sister and that's why Lucy's ghost killed someone every nineteen years. Even after death, she was trying to get payback for what her sister had done.

It made sense. A pattern for something that might have been random. I frowned. I hated the thoughts Anson had put there, however well-meaning. I was doubting myself too much.

I went back to my internet search on how to get rid of ghosts. Given that Lucy had disappeared, I wondered if I'd need to find her body and give her a real burial. Maybe I needed to write up the truth about her life. I certainly couldn't kill her sister for her.

I found little practical help in my search. Nothing even touched on the possibility of a ghost trying to kill a living person. In my reading, it seemed like most ghost experts didn't believe such a thing was possible. Clearly, none of them had visited Steely Woods rest stop.

A few sites suggested returning to the place of the original crime. I had the vacation time and Nils wasn't likely to balk at letting me take it now.

I looked up and stared around the Starbucks. The tables had filled while I researched ghosts and more people were waiting to order. Others stood together, waiting for their drinks to be finished. There was plenty of life.

My phone chimed letting me know I had a text.

Anson. Which surprised me.

"Will and I want to chat."

"When and where," I typed.

"When you free?"

"I'm at Starbucks." I added the street in case they didn't know which one. There aren't as many here as there were in the Northwest but there were still plenty of them.

"Fifteen minutes."

Which gave me fifteen minutes to worry about what they might have to say and why they both wanted to see me. Anson and I had seen something horrible but Will hadn't. Will had been intrigued by Deborah's story about the murder in Steely Woods, though, and I wondered how much Anson had taken him into his confidence.

The man in the corner got up and left, taking his computer with him. Whatever work had brought him out on a Saturday morning was finished.

I watched as an older woman placed her order. She clearly wasn't used to all the choices and the barista had to explain several of them. I admired the patience with which the woman behind the counter spoke. The line got longer while the girl talked. I felt my shoulders tensing just thinking about how the barista must feel knowing she was falling further and further behind.

A second helper came to the other cash register, probably noticing that the line was starting to push against the door.

Maybe I should have asked Anson and Will if they wanted anything.

I watched people, letting my mind wander until the two men came in. Both were already carrying Starbucks cups. Anson had a venti something in a clear plastic glass and Will had a smaller cup of something hot, probably black coffee, which was what he usually got when he was working.

"You already stopped here?" I asked.

"We met up at the Harris Teeter in my neighborhood," Will said, looking mostly at the floor. "Once we started talking, Anson said you ought to be involved."

Will wore loose fitting jeans and a Panther's shirt. Anson also wore jeans and his shirt was a plain red t-shirt. Both men looked casual. Will looked more rested than Anson but not by much, which surprised me.

"So what's up?" I asked, leaning forward.

There was only one other chair. Will looked around uncomfortably until Anson asked the woman next to us if we could borrow the chair from her table. She nodded it was fine so he settled in. Music swirled around us. Three coworkers just discussing life. Normal.

Except it wasn't.

"I didn't sleep well," Will said, starting. "I emailed Anson really early this morning about the nightmares I kept having and the things they brought up. I keep seeing Deborah going to that rest stop in Washington and the thing following her, like it noticed her there. I was terrified, but I was just watching so I couldn't do anything."

I wanted to be sympathetic and it's not that I wasn't, but my dreams were so much worse, I didn't really know what to say.

"I got his email and said that you had been attacked at that rest stop and maybe it was following you," Anson jumped in.

"That made sense to me," Will said. "I've spent the morning researching stuff. You wouldn't believe what I found out."

I waited.

Anson was practically ready to jump out of his seat. I wondered what could be so interesting.

"When they were building the rest stop, they found a body, well, skeleton. No one knows who it was or why she was there. There were some rumors that it could be a girl who went missing over a decade before, Lucy Martin, but no one knows for certain. Lucy had a sister but the sister died before they thought to take DNA or anything." Will talked quickly, almost excitedly, but he kept his eyes on his coffee, as if it were more interested in his story than Anson and me.

I was stunned. "I've been working on researching this for I don't know how long. I've been over the history of that rest stop and I never found anything about the bones." I was mad. I'd worked so hard. How had Will found something like that?

"I started looking for bones found when things were being built anywhere in the area. There's no way to know whether this has anything to do with the girl who went missing because the area was an old field then and it's not like they had DNA when the rest stop was built," Will said.

I nodded. I hadn't considered that angle of research. I'd been focused on the place.

"What made you decide to search those key terms?" I took a sip of coffee. Maybe Will and Anson would see things I didn't. I'd avoided horror movies and scary novels. The two men, by contrast, seemed fascinated by death, though both were clearly rethinking their interest.

"I guess it was the dream and believing Deborah's killer was a ghost. The most common reason for a ghost to haunt a place would be because they'd been murdered there," Will said. His face pinked ever so slightly.

"But ghosts that kill people?" I asked.

Will shrugged, head down.

"There are poltergeists," Anson said. "I read up on hauntings that seemed more forceful and some experts think those aren't really ghosts but demons. I guess they have more abilities in our world."

"I can give you ghosts, maybe," I said, "I saw something terrifying at Steely Woods and I don't think it was natural. I think it was something supernatural. But this thing looked like a rotting body. Then it was gone. I don't think that's what a demon looks like. Is it?"

I hadn't read up on demons. Maybe they weren't the cloven hoofed things I had in my imagination.

Will nodded. "I don't believe it's a demon either. That's so Hollywood. Maybe it is possible for someone who died to influence and take from the living if there was enough negative emotion attached to their death...at least that's how I interpret some of what I've read."

Anson looked skeptical.

"You don't think so?" I asked Anson.

He shrugged and then sipped his drink. "I think a ghost is an easy way to make sense of what happened. I'm not sure I can really go for the whole supernatural thing. It felt that way when I was there, you know. So weird. No one around. I can't believe I couldn't have heard anything from a person and you would have had to see someone." Anson held my gaze. "But there wasn't anyone, except maybe the one truck driver, which I haven't heard anything more about."

"Maybe we can call?" I had the card from one of the detectives, something in case I remembered anything.

Anson shrugged. "I can't say I believe in the supernatural. Not really. If there were ghosts wouldn't more people know about them? Wouldn't they be more prevalent? This doesn't make sense."

Will sighed. "My mother believed in ghosts and I swear I saw my aunt the day she died, coming to give my mother a hug. My mom turned, like she knew she was there and then nothing. We got the call a few hours later but my mom already knew. She started crying the minute the phone rang."

"Maybe you remember it that way because you want to," Anson said.

I started to say something, to ask him about his apparent belief the other day.

"I know," he told me before I could get the words out. "I latched onto the supernatural thing. It's what makes sense for my brain. But I know it's just my brain trying to make sense of something that it doesn't understand. It's like the people who started worshipping gods. God was a way to make sense of things they didn't understand. I think this stuff is like that too."

"Maybe what we don't understand is the supernatural," Will said. "I've had experiences. Traci has had at least one. Something happened to Deborah and a human doesn't make sense."

"And why did that thing follow Traci?" Anson asked. "Because she got away? Then why didn't it take her. It makes no sense."

"You acted like you believed," I said. I had shared stuff, vulnerable stuff with him. He hadn't laughed.

"Our minds are amazing," Anson said. "I think they fill in things when life is complicated. For all of us, the supernatural is the easiest way to fill in the blank. Even you with the skeletal figure. Was it really skeletal? Could it have been human, maybe in costume? The girls came in and the person fled. You think it just disappeared. Maybe they rushed out, pulling off the costume."

Anson hadn't been there. He hadn't felt the danger. I had. I wasn't paranoid then. I didn't jump every time a faucet dripped. No one who hadn't been through what I had been through could understand. I knew I was going to die in that moment.

Will shrugged, looking at Anson. "Then maybe you don't need to be part of this."

"But you might come up with something that will help me explain why Deborah is dead," Anson said. His voice was almost shaking. He needed something to let him understand what had happened but he couldn't go whole heartedly into the supernatural thing.

"I was thinking I need to go back there," I said. My voice may have shaken a little too.

"That's probably true if she's following you," Will said.

Anson said nothing.

"I was there late, after midnight. There wasn't anyone else there, at least not in any of the buildings. I think there might have been a couple of truckers outside, probably asleep. I remember traffic being light even on the freeway before I turned off."

Will nodded, encouraging.

"I probably have to go there at night."

"And probably alone," Will said, looking at my face, completely out of character.

"Do you think?" I asked. I didn't want to be alone. I had hoped he'd volunteer to come along.

"What was the date you were at the rest stop? Was it exactly nineteen years before?"

"I was there in spring. So it would have been just over nineteen years. I saw that Lucy Martin had a sister and she'd have been nineteen when Lucy disappeared," I added. "I thought maybe the nineteen was the age of her sister. Maybe her sister had something to do with Lucy's disappearance."

"So now we're solving a cold case that's nearly a hundred years old?" Anson asked. His voice was a bit louder. The woman Will had borrowed a chair from looked over at him. Even the barista looked up at what he said, although with the music and the other voices, I didn't believe she'd actually heard the words, just the tone.

"It's all part of the puzzle," I said. "We're trying to make sense of this and the next piece is apparently in the past. What if Lucy's death did have something to do with the deaths at the rest stop?"

Will was nodding. "If her sister murdered her, I could see her being so pissed off that she'd want to murder people even after death. Maybe that anger gives enough power to actually do it, kind of like a demon."

"You'd think if they found her bones that she'd be more at rest." Anson leaned back and crossed his arms as if that was the final say.

"What if those bones weren't hers?" I asked.

Even Will looked a little surprised, but then he smiled grimly and nodded.

20

TRACI: SEPTEMBER NOW

We talked for perhaps an hour. Anson had less and less to say as Will and I bounced ideas off of each other. The two of them left, Anson going in one direction and Will in another. Although they had arrived together, they'd come from meeting each other at another Starbucks.

I left not long after they did. The silence of my condo seemed to echo around me after having had a discussion in the coffee shop. I didn't often listen to music at home any longer, lest I miss a sound, but I missed the background noise of Starbucks. Still, I didn't move to turn on the television or a radio. I was too alone and not yet ready to test my ability to make out the sound of a single drip while music played.

I settled at my table and enjoyed the brightness. The sun filtered through gray clouds that hovered low over the city. We were in for a storm. I had all my lights burning, including my lanterns. When the storm came, it wouldn't be silent in the apartment any longer. I waited for thunder.

After talking to Will, I decided I'd ask Nils for the latter half of the week off and all of the next one. I'd be taking ten vacation days. I could stay in Portland. I sent emails to a couple of old friends, including Ronette, who I'd been up visiting when I'd stopped at that rest stop.

We'd drifted apart when I'd moved, but we'd been roommates in college. It was her April birthday that we'd been celebrating when I'd stopped at Steely Woods at two in the morning and nearly died. I wondered how she'd have felt if I had died.

Ronette had been as supportive as anyone, but given that I wouldn't drive up to see her after the incident made it harder to keep in touch. Sure, she drove down, but it's a fairly long drive and when I wouldn't reciprocate or fully explain why, I think she thought I didn't care about our friendship. Facebook had helped draw us back together but we'd never be as close as we'd once been.

I made a few other plans and sent Nils a note about what I hoped to do. I wanted confirmation from him that it would be fine before I actually booked plane tickets, though I had researched those along with hotels.

There wasn't any place to stay close to Steely Woods, so I needed to decide where to stay. I poured over the map until I got a note from Nils saying that I could take the time off. I wasted no time in booking tickets to Portland.

I got a hotel in Portland. I could drive north past Steely Woods and then turn around and come south to reach the rest stop where it had happened. Hopefully, I'd live to see the hotel another night.

I sent Will a message. Even if I had to do this alone, I wanted someone to know the timing of my plans. Assuming I made it through confronting the ghost, I'd head up to Tacoma to see Ronette after that.

I searched around on the internet trying to figure out what might have happened to Lucy, but found nothing. I did find one of those cold case forums and I input her name. Even there, I found no mention.

The forum seemed like a likely place for answers. I set up a new email under a false name. I wasn't ready to out myself completely. Then I set up an account and posted my question. I'd wait and see if I got any information or answers. Maybe I'd get a lead.

Too bad they didn't have forums like that for ghost hunting and getting rid of ghosts. I hadn't thought to look but as soon as I found the crime forum, I did a search for ghost hunting forums. There were places people talked about ghosts but nothing on how to get rid of one. From the conversations, I doubted I'd be taken seriously at those.

At some point, the rain started. I turned when it started tapping on the window, surprised. The light had dimmed, but with all the overheads on and my lanterns on, it still wasn't shadowed. Time had flown with all my searching and planning.

I paused, listening.

There was only the tap tap of the rain on the window.

I got up and made some macaroni for dinner. It wasn't fancy but I'm not a fancy eater. I made a salad to eat while the water boiled. In television shows people who lived alone often made scrumptious meals for themselves and sat down at a table with a bowl of salad and a main meal all ready to go. I wasn't one of those people. I was lucky to think about making salad and then only because I heard my mother's voice in my head making me feel guilty for not having it.

So I ate my salad while the pasta heated and then I melted some cheese for the sauce.

I turned on the television and actually watched something for a change. It had been over a week since I had turned it on. I'd been too busy listening for the telltale drip of a faucet.

Maybe Lucy was pleased that I was going to go search her out. Or maybe she was just eager to get me in her own place, to take my soul to her wherever she rested.

Will texted me back as I was finishing dinner. I had forgotten that I'd let him know my plans. He wanted to call and chat.

I told him now was a good time.

I lowered the television volume and waited to see if he would be prompt. He was.

"I'm sorry it took so long to get back to you. After talking to you and Anson, who I'm sort of pissed at, but never mind, I went to a friend's house. His wife is an energy healer and they're into all this woo woo stuff and we started talking about things and trolling the net trying to find answers," Will said. He was nearly breathless.

"And you found something?" It was clear from his tone that whatever it was, he thought it was important.

"We found the same general information you found about Lucy and Alma, I think. I also found out that before the rest stop was there, drivers used to think they saw a girl in ripped clothing running out onto the freeway trying to flag someone down. It sounds like an urban legend but there was an interview on a ghost site from some older man who said he'd actually seen it."

Which was interesting, if it were true. It was hard to say after all this time.

"Why do you suppose she stopped running out there?" I played with my hair a little, frowning, though he couldn't see me. The story didn't seem all that relevant.

"The thing is, I guess a girl was picked up there after running out onto the highway in her nightgown. She claimed a man nearly killed her. Unfortunately, she was too incoherent for the police to get much out of her. Given the time period, I don't know how hard they tried. She ended up at Western State, which I guess was a mental hospital."

As far as I knew it still was. Which meant our girl wasn't Lucy.

"It couldn't have been Lucy, then, could it? Because she's dead, if she's the girl I'm seeing."

"This woman died after a couple of years at Western State. I couldn't find anything out. And no one had her name."

Great. I could be fighting with a ghost who wasn't even there.

"So let me get this straight. We have at least one set of bones buried where they built the rest stop, a ghost of a woman running out onto the freeway, a woman who was nearly killed who actually did run out into the freeway and died while she was at Western State miles to the north. We also have Lucy, who might or might not have been the bones buried in the rest stop or the girl who was picked up by the driver."

"Exactly," Will said. It was like he was a teacher pleased that the student had gotten the answer right, although what was the right answer here? "Think about it. Today if a woman tried to flag down a trucker after another woman had gone missing in the area, the police would start connecting the dots. Maybe a serial killer."

"Did anyone else go missing around there?" I asked.

"Can't find anything." Will didn't sound very unhappy about it. "But it was 1942 and Lucy was considered a prosti-tute. So was her sister. The woman at Western States was never reported missing and they only have a first name, Jenny. No one identified her. In fact, from the stories I read, Jenny might not even have been her name. It was just the name she kept repeating over and over again. For all we know, Jenny might be the bones that were found. Maybe she saw Lucy or Lucy saw her."

"Do we know when Jenny ran out onto the freeway?" I asked.

"The stories say in the fifties," Will said. "So maybe she saw Lucy."

I bit my lip. "I signed up for one those cold case investigator websites under a false name. In case someone came up with anything."

"Have they?" Now there was more excitement from Will.

"I haven't checked back. It was only a couple of hours ago. I figure it will take some time. It's not like she's a famous missing person. I'll check in tomorrow."

"Sounds like a great plan. My friends think it's a good idea you're going back there. You need to finish this."

"Did they have any advice for finishing it?" That was what I needed.

"Take any silver jewelry you have. Also, if you have a favorite religion that brings comfort, take any symbols of that. They like salt for protection. Doesn't matter which kind, although Ani, the wife, tends to prefer a Celtic or Himalayan Sea Salt because she thinks it's more natural than iodized. She admits any type will do, though."

I could purchase salt in Portland. I wasn't going to take a huge package of it in my suitcase. I had some silver earrings and a bracelet, but other than that I had no silver jewelry. Mentally I wondered if taking a cross necklace would help. I'd been raised in the Lutheran church, rather haphazardly, going now and again, but mostly not. When I left home, I'd gone to church a few times. After the incident, I went for about six months regularly but got no comfort or answers from it. In fact, the minister was one of the first to suggest therapy.

"But how do I confront the ghost?"

"You'll need to go back to the place it happened and hope she shows up. If this was related to Deborah's death, then she'll probably come if you're in her space. Just be prepared."

"So I have things to protect me, what do I do next?"

"Ani suggested chanting be gone. I guess it's not so much the words as much as your intent. Also a knife to cut the binding between you two, maybe make a rope or something symbolic to disentangle yourselves. Ani says you're in a unique position to possibly help people later on. I mean if you just cut that cord, so to speak, then this ghost goes back to what she was doing. Maybe she doesn't bother you but in another nineteen years, she could kill again. Tied to you, you have the ability to destroy her."

Except I didn't know how.

"Any advice on that? Besides telling her to leave, which is kind of like telling the wolf that's standing on my chest drooling to be a nice doggy, don't you think?" I hated to be snide and sarcastic, but Will seemed to take it okay. He laughed a little before answering.

"Unfortunately, no, they didn't have any advice. You could try a silver knife or if you find something sharp in iron that might work. If you have access to holy water, you could dip the knife in that before you go. Or have a priest or someone bless the object."

I didn't know anyone I could call on to bless a sharp object. I suppose I could walk into a random Catholic Church, but I had concerns about being able to walk out again on my own. "Why silver or iron?"

"Ani said that iron has historically been used against supernatural creatures. Silver came into a fad in the 1930s in the movies. She's not certain how protective it is, but she always advises using it, just in case. Iron has a longer history of being anathema to faeries and other creatures that could harm someone. It doesn't actually work against ghosts but we're not completely sure that this creature is really a ghost or if it's something else. Ghosts can't normally hurt someone, which Ani says means it might have turned into some other sort of supernatural creature and iron typically works against them."

Not that silver or iron knives were easy to find. I didn't even know where to start searching for such a thing, something I mentioned to Will.

He thought about it. "I think you could probably find a place setting for a silver set in an antique store and maybe use a knife sharpener to sharpen a silver knife. I'm not sure about iron."

I got up and went to my computer and started searching while Will talked about the ways in which I might find silver that wasn't too expensive and some that were, like buying real silver and melting it down. Like I had the time and money for that.

Google let me know that steel is iron so if I got steel nails they might work. And they were naturally sharp. I could probably use a lot of different gardening tools too. Easier than I thought. Stainless steel would probably be iron of a type, too, which was what my flatware was made of.

"Ani also said you could do a banishing ritual. The "be gone" chant would be part of it, or whatever speaks to you," Will said. "She suggested getting something that belonged to Lucy or at least something that represents the ghost to you. Burn it near the rest stop, if you can. Then take the iron knife and do a symbolic cut on the cord that ties you to it. Put your energy into making sure that you think of the spirit being gone. If she is buried around the rest stop and wasn't found, finding her bones and giving her a consecrated burial would be best. If not, cut a symbolic cord between her and the rest stop."

"That's a lot," I said, trying to remember everything. Will

began listing herbs to take as well and which I ought to try burning during the ritual.

"I'll send you an email. Ani has it all worked out for me. You'd need help finding the bones, but I'm not sure what. I researched cadaver dogs for you, but the body would still need to have enough tissue to smell. Lucy disappeared too long ago for that to happen easily, although some cadaver dogs are that good," Will said.

"An email would be helpful. I wonder how police do it when looking for bones?"

"Ground penetrating radar. If you know someone who has it, great, but it doesn't look like something you buy easily. I mean, I suppose if you had a ton of money you could get it. But even then, it's not foolproof. If Lucy is only partly there, only a part of a skeleton, then the radar might not catch it, especially if the bones weren't grouped super close together."

I rolled my eyes. Will was taking this far too seriously. Did he think I'd go on to rent a backhoe too, to dig up land that was probably owned by the state or the highway system or something?

Finally, Will rang off, promising to send me the email soon. I wondered if perhaps he was too eager. Maybe I should have listened to Anson.

I sighed, stretching my neck. I could go back to the sofa and watch some more television. As I got up, I saw a shadow moving in the bathroom. Vaguely human shaped, though too thin to be normal. A clawed hand reached out along one wall, like it was pulling itself out of the room.

My heart pounded and my breath shortened. I had thought I was done with Lucy. Instead she was back, apparently more powerful than ever.

LUCY: EARLY FALL THEN

Lucy tugged at the door of the trailer. She'd gotten up that morning, intending to go town, maybe school. Maybe she'd even have talked to someone about her sister, but Alma had been up first and when she'd left, she'd locked the door.

The place stunk because Alma hadn't emptied the toilet before leaving. Lucy needed to go but she wasn't keen on going into the small bathroom with the partially full bucket.

Outside, wind rattled the trailer. Lucy felt like she was in a giant creaking and groaning body, unable to escape.

She looked at the windows. The small ones opened. The largest of them was over the little seating area in the back of the trailer, by the table. She crawled onto the bench that ran under it and tried to open the thing. It squealed. Wind gusted in, blowing her hair back. She shivered. It wasn't that cold, but the wind bit into her body sending the slight chill deep into her bones.

No screen blocked her way as all of them had long since disappeared from the trailer, if it had ever had them. Unfortunately, the window only opened a little ways from top to bottom and that wasn't quite wide enough for her to get her shoulders through.

Lucy debated about breaking it and making a run for it. But then she'd have to remain on the run. It probably meant telling someone what she'd done, what Alma had done.

Lucy climbed up to her bunk and began putting a few things in a pillowcase to more easily carry them. She searched through the small bedroom and under the bunk, going through Alma's things, even the lacy underwear that was placed nicely in a drawer. Everything else was scattered around.

Some coins fell out of corners and crannies, and in the bottom drawer, Lucy found two twenties tucked away. She smiled. She pocketed that. She grabbed her coat. Then she tossed the pillow case and the coat out the window and pushed herself out.

The hinges on the window were harder to break than she expected. Her hands got tired of pushing, feeling achy. Her palms had a red line across them from where it had pressed against the window. Lucy watched her jacket slide under the trailer with the next gust of wind. She hoped that it didn't blow out the other side and fly into the woods.

Lucy gritted her teeth and gave the window another push. Her hands banged against the side of the trailer when the window gave way, sending a shock up her arms. It took a moment before the ache dissipated and she could pull herself up and partly through the window. Only then did she realize she'd be falling out headfirst. Lucy slid back in the trailer and stood up and put a leg out first, angling herself to go out that way. She had to sit on the window and lean back, almost touching the table before she was able to slip through.

Her breasts connected with the top of the window and she had to push herself down and through, scraping the front of her body, tearing away the thin fabric of her shirt

Lucy swore silently and cursed Alma.

Finally, her breasts cleared the narrow part of the window and she was free. Her coat had caught on a brick where the trailer was raised. Lucy grabbed it and pulled it on. Then she took her pillowcase and made for the trail in the woods to town. Hopefully, someone would help her.

2 2

TRACI: SEPTEMBER NOW

My nose twitched at the metallic smell that slammed into me like a physical thing. Old blood and rotting meat. I nearly gagged up the air that I had finally managed to take in.

I heard nothing, not a single drip of a faucet. I backed up towards the wall of my condo on legs that could barely stand. I slipped down to a crouched position, shaking, my arms up in front of me, not quite daring to cover my eyes.

The shadow moved out of the bathroom, along a wall. I could barely see it because of the angle. Then, even from where I sat, I saw a hand reach out of the little room down the hall.

I think I sobbed a little.

Thunder crashed outside and rain began again in earnest.

I waited for the lights to go out, to feel the slim cold fingers of bone against the back of my neck or perhaps sliding down my cheekbone.

My imagination ran wild with ideas, my heart pumping faster and faster like a train chugging along up a hill far too fast.

A door slammed out in the corridor.

I jumped.

The shadow disappeared.

I remained where I was, crouching in the corner, just waiting for something else to happen. My ears strained for sounds that didn't come. My eyes stayed on the hall searching for any sign of a shadow moving.

I sat there, eyes wide, frozen in fear for a very long time. Did rabbits wait that long when they sensed a predator? I read once that the best defense was out-wait the predator. It's why cats were successful. They had the patience to stalk. I wondered how much patience my ghost had, imaging it sitting back in the bathroom, waiting for me to walk past, to jump out, to grab me.

I wanted to giggle suddenly when I realized there was no reason for her not to be patient. She was dead. She had all the time in the world. She could corner me there in my breakfast nook and keep me from doing anything. She could leave me to sit there until I died from lack of food and water.

How quickly one's bravery falls to the wayside when confronted with one's own mortality.

At some point I began chewing on my thumb, still waiting. My thumbnail gone, I had to move on to another nail.

My bladder filled faster than time passed. I would need to move soon.

Still I waited.

When my legs began to cramp, I slowly pushed myself up along the wall. Nothing moved down the hall. No strange forms waited for me. No shadows danced along the walls.

Even so, I stood in the breakfast nook mentally preparing myself to walk down the hall, to look into the bathroom, perhaps even to use the toilet.

Any sound of cars passing along the road outside disappeared from my consciousness. Now it was me and the periodic tap of rain. Someone started running water, whether a toilet flush or a dishwasher, probably from downstairs.

I took one hesitant step forward.

Nothing jumped out at me. No faucet dripped.

Gaining confidence, I took another and then soon enough I was across the kitchen and standing at the opening to the hallway.

No shadows. The lights remained on. All of them.

I walked down the hall and peered into my bathroom.

Nothing.

I breathed out. It would take a long time for my heart to slow, but for now, I felt safe enough.

I went in to use the toilet.

No faucet dripped. No skeletal hand threatened to pull aside the clear shower curtain to reveal a creature I'd run from years ago. I finished, still alive, though my hands may have shaken just a bit as I flushed.

I made the mistake of looking in the mirror while washing my hands.

There, I saw a skull, grinning teeth, one broken eye socket, four stray hairs still sticking to the top of the rounded bone. Three teeth were gone. The curve on the right looked wrong, as if the bones were broken. The skull was attached to a boney neck, a scrap of blue cloth still sticking to it.

Over it, my face was superimposed, almost exactly.

I stumbled back, feeling the warmth of the wall.

I screamed as loudly and as long as I could. I no longer worried about bothering the neighbors. I wanted them to wonder what was happening. Wanted someone to hear and perhaps call the police.

"Come to me, one that got away, and I'll tell you my secrets." The voice was soft and slightly scratchy and sounded as if it were on a long distance, perhaps a transcontinental 1950s phone call.

My screams hitched and I started to hyperventilate.

"Kill him for me and I'll let you go." The voice was stronger, as if it was getting used to speaking again.

The skull in the mirror was gone.

Still I couldn't help but squeak out, "What if he's dead?" I'd done the math. If Alma hadn't killed Lucy and someone else had, chances were they were over a hundred. Not likely to be still alive.

"Then I'll take you in his place," the voice said.

I shivered and slid down towards the floor, a fist in my mouth.

Which was where I stayed, staring at the cabinet that held the sink in front of me until daylight came again.

My heart rate still hadn't slowed.

TRACI: SEPTEMBER NOW

I didn't know exactly when Sunday dawned. I was on the floor of the bathroom, staring at the sink cabinet, my eyes gritty, my mind tired, and my muscles stiff from not moving all night. If asked, I couldn't say if I had blinked, though I must have as I don't think you can go for hours without doing so.

My heart still pounded far too hard, though it had slowed, and I could draw a breath, but each time I did, I worried that I was being overheard.

At some point, I slipped out of the bathroom, avoiding looking into the mirror again, though I knew that Lucy was gone.

No shadows lurked, waiting to grab me. No faucets dripped. Upstairs, the neighbors bounced around and I heard a vacuum cleaner running, a soft purr that was perhaps the sound that soothed me enough to get up and move. Fortunately, my neighbors cleaned early on a Sunday. I was probably the only person in the world grateful for that.

I poured myself some orange juice, letting the sweet acidity of it perk me up a bit. I find orange juice disappointing in that it never smells as good as a fresh orange though I like the taste. It's something that I puzzle over from time to time. Why does the juice not smell as good as the orange itself?

The thought was a great distraction and about as much as my exhausted mind could handle.

I tumbled into bed and napped restlessly in the daylight for a few hours before getting up to go back to researching. I was hesitant to contact Will. After all, maybe thinking about the mystery so much was forcing me into insanity. Even if I wasn't actually losing touch with reality, I worried Will might think that's exactly what was happening.

I certainly couldn't tell Anson about my experience. It was one thing to share that I'd had a bad experience in a rest stop and that I jumped at shadows because of that. That might be a normal sort of PTSD thing. He could handle that.

Seeing a ghostly face in the bathroom mirror and having it threaten you was not normal. Not by any standards. I doubted he'd even question my sanity. I might find men in white coats waiting for me before I left town.

I set the glass in the sink and looked around the condo. I opened the blinds, something I normally did first thing every morning. My electricity bill was enormous, but I didn't do much socializing. It averaged out. Periodically I was ashamed that I wasn't doing my part, so to speak, for the planet, but that was neither here nor there.

I breathed in. My flight didn't leave until Wednesday. I had two days of work before heading off to Washington. I could get back in my routine, a little bit, and see how things went. I rubbed my eyes, feeling tears. If I couldn't sleep, though, how would I ever have a normal day at work?

My stomach tied itself in knots as I worried how I'd get through those days. I couldn't even tell anyone what I was going through because they'd think I'd finally lost it. Then, someone might even call the mental health professionals to lock me up in a hospital. A hospital that might not care how bright the lights were, where they might even force me to try and sleep in the dark. What if I wasn't crazy—and mostly I was certain I wasn't—and she came for me?

I wondered how afraid Deborah had been. Had she believed what she saw? Had she been as terrified as I was? Did she hurt? Had Lucy told her why?

I didn't think Lucy would have spoken. She didn't speak to me at all, the one time I saw her.

Finally I went to my phone and called Will.

"Hey," he said picking up on the second ring.

"I hope I'm not bothering you but I had a question," I said.

"Shoot." Will sounded like he was eating something. It was probably a late lunch or maybe a snack. Or maybe he was watching the game.

"What if Lucy's goal is to get revenge and kill her killer and he's dead?"

"Maybe telling her he's dead?" Will suggested.

"What if that's not enough?"

"That's harder. Maybe you can locate any relatives who are still alive and let them know what their relative did?" Will sounded thoughtful. "I don't know. Normally, just knowing the murderer is dead offers some peace. Or if there's a medium, maybe they can get the two to communicate?"

I made some conciliatory comments, though I was wondering how he expected me to find people like that. I didn't know a medium. Who said, "Oh yes, a medium. Of course. I'll check my contacts because I know several and I'll see who's available."

I hung up, frustrated. But I got on the computer and went to the cold case forum. I'd made my screen name "Lucy-Friend," though I doubted if Lucy thought of me as a friend.

It was better than "HauntedTraci" which might eventually lead someone to me.

I checked my post and one person called SerialHunter had responded with a generic comment about needing more information.

WAFinder gave me one of the websites Will had found and commented interesting.

That started a discussion with someone name Pit saying the bones probably belonged to someone other than Lucy. DNA would help if there were any relatives still alive.

I didn't know if there were relatives or where to find out if there were. WAFinder was also unable to find any living relatives, though he or she had found Alma. Alma had not had children, at least not that either of us had located.

Pit was certain the bones hadn't belonged to Lucy. I still wondered.

WAFinder didn't seem convinced.

SerialHunter said that the only way to be sure would be to search the area for more bones. He didn't specify how.

WAFinder had a search and rescue dog, but it had a good nose and had periodically found bones. He or she offered to meet me there.

So now I had to decide if I trusted this person I only knew online to meet me at a rest stop along I-5 to search for bones. I'd be alone, really alone, and there was no one I could take with me, unless Ronette agreed to be there. I couldn't see that happening, but then again, I hadn't asked.

I went onto Facebook and sent her a note. I let her know I was trying to work through my terror of Steely Woods and wondered if she'd come with me. I left out, for the moment, that I might be meeting another person there, one with a dog that was supposed to be search and rescue. Even thinking about meeting them was probably stupid.

I sent the note anyway, thinking I could extricate us both

if things sounded really sketchy. I contacted WAFinder via PM on the forum and started asking further questions.

WAFinder said her real name was Lois Neil. Her dog, which she used as a picture, was a black standard poodle named Mercedes. She said noonish would be good as she would drive down from Puyallup.

I looked her up on other social media sites and the photo image was the same. Her profiles also held personal images of a woman perhaps fifteen years older than I was, with graying hair. There were more photos of the dog and a few of young children who were probably her grandchildren. She loved reading, mostly mysteries, and she belonged to several Facebook groups on solving cold case mysteries. She was even a member of a group devoted to psychics.

"I'll bring my husband along," she wrote. "He's not much into this but doesn't like me meeting strangers alone."

Well good for him. I didn't like it much either.

"If I can come, I'll bring a friend." I didn't tell her Ronette was a woman. I'd leave her to think I was bringing a boyfriend or someone like that.

I bit my lip. I hoped this worked out. I'd have people around me at the rest stop. If I had to go back alone at night, at least I'd know what I was getting into. The day wouldn't be wasted.

I breathed in and watched the cars driving by on the street for a few minutes. I didn't quite feel safe but I felt as if I had a reprieve, though I was dreading the night. What would happen then?

I decided that seeing I had food in the house and I wasn't terribly hungry, I'd shower before the sun went down. I'd need to use the bathroom after dark but at least I'd be clean and not getting up in the near dark to shower in the morning. One less thing to worry about. I could sleep in a little longer if the ghost reappeared and kept me awake again.

All that drove me to tears, realizing how limited my life was. How had I survived like that for so long without questioning things? It had taken a coworker to die and a ramping up of the haunting to make me realize how boxed in my life had become.

That had to change. One way or another. As I had no desire to die, wasn't planning on dying, I needed to survive my encounter with Lucy. Another week and this could be over. At least I hoped so.

24

TRACI SEPTEMBER NOW

I didn't sleep much Sunday night and I was thankful when Monday morning rolled around. I had lain looking towards the doorway all night and my neck had stiffened up. My bladder felt ready to burst because I'd been too afraid to get out of the bed until dawn. I hadn't dreamed, probably because I'd just dozed my way through the night.

This was similar to what I'd gone through shortly after the attack. I'd been too afraid to sleep because dreams of that clawed hand reached out for me, grasping a cupboard, or perhaps sneaking up behind the sofa would have me waking in terror. It had taken months before I could do more than doze my way through the night.

I'd slowly gotten better, getting a decent night's sleep at least half the time. Months went by when I'd be okay and then other weeks when I wouldn't sleep hardly at all. The time in between I would sleep, but be torn apart by nightmares.

Someone in my building made bacon for breakfast and the smell reached me even in my bed. I didn't have an appetite, and the idea of something that greasy made my stomach feel queasy, though normally I liked bacon.

I sat on the edge of my bed, covering my face. I had plenty of time to waste, particularly if breakfast held no appeal. Slowly I pushed myself through an abbreviated morning routine, checking and double checking shadows around me, avoiding looking in the bathroom mirror.

I arrived at work only a few minutes early. Around me the underground parking garage was swathed in its normal amount of shadows. I drew in a breath and let it out as I sat in the car. I hadn't ever seen Lucy in my car. As a result, I felt reasonably safe there, though I'd never tried sleeping there. The safety I felt inside the car disappeared the moment I turned off the engine, when I was no longer able to flee if Lucy turned up.

Although it was early, the sun was up, not quite all the way. Getting out, I felt the humidity and heat. The day was already starting out warm. You'd think with all the sunshine and heat that ghosts wouldn't like the South, but oddly, in my reading, the South was one of the more haunted places in the United States. Given that Lucy seemed to want to appear only when I was alone, I would have thought a city that bustled with 13 million people would be safe. I had no idea what kind of a beacon I was to the ghost and how she kept finding me, but somehow she did. I needed to destroy her before she completely destroyed me.

Having a plan to deal with my fears allowed me to work a little more effectively that day. I wasn't at my best, but I got through my emails and worked on some things that needed to be taken care of, particularly if I was leaving for a few days.

Anson came in and stood over my desk.

"Yes?" I asked.

"You're still going out there?" he asked.

"I am," I said.

He shifted from foot to foot. Finally, "I think it's good you're going back to where you were attacked. I hope you'll give up the idea of it being something supernatural. It's one thing to consider that, to mull over it, but it's not something you can believe in, you know?"

"No." I leaned back looking at him. "I don't know. I'm particularly confused because you were the one leading me down the path of believing in the supernatural and now that I'm willing to consider it, to go with it, you're telling me I shouldn't. Which is it?"

"I like to play with ideas. It's not like they're all possible. It seems like what happened to Deborah has no answer because we didn't see anything, but there has to be a mundane sort of thing. The guy went out the window or something, like I said Saturday morning. I can't believe you and Will were even talking about spells to banish ghosts. At least you could have called a minister to do it for you if you had to go that route."

"Is that the issue? Spells?" I couldn't get a handle on where Anson was coming from.

"Look, I don't know what you saw at that rest stop when you were attacked. Only you know, but it had to be someone who was killing people. There were other deaths there, you know. It may be some sort of initiation into a cult so you thought you saw something. Deborah was just in the wrong place at the wrong time. Her death had nothing to do with the supernatural. Maybe it was another woman who killed her. A small woman could have gone out that window."

A very small woman, I thought. And a fast one, too, because she'd killed Deborah and then gotten out and closed the window behind her. I wasn't going to argue with Anson.

"So you're here to tell me that if I believe all the stuff you said the other day I'm crazy? I shouldn't believe your crazy rantings because it's okay for you to toss off ideas but not the rest of us?"

"No," Anson said. He looked really uncomfortable. "I just want you to know that I said what I did because I was stressed. It's logical for the brain to try and find a way to explain the unexplainable, okay? I couldn't. I still can't. The supernatural is the easy out. I think you're better than that and I'll feel badly if you suddenly start believing in ghosts and stuff because I ran my mouth off. I can't believe how much people seem to want to think it exists. Will is completely into this in ways that I couldn't even begin to imagine and he wasn't even there."

Anson still didn't make sense to me. "So you're mostly worried that you suggested I believe something that had never occurred to me before? Or encouraged me in believing in something you think is crazy, right?" I hoped I wasn't being insulting.

"I guess," Anson said. He looked around at the office. He hadn't stopped dancing around as he spoke. "I was also hoping to be a voice of reason because I'm worried about what you and Will have planned. It's crazy to think that any sort of ritual will help. I mean, I know it might make you feel better, but if you've been carrying around your terror for that long, it's not going away because of a ritual. You'll need to see someone who understands this kind of thing and talk to them."

"Thanks for your advice," I said. "I have talked to people. And nothing has ever made sense out of this. The supernatural is as likely a reason as anything. I appreciate your support when Deborah died, but I'm doing what I need to do. I'm a big girl."

Anson didn't look at all cowed. He just nodded and left. I was fuming. I had thought he was an ally and then just when I had confided something to him, he had become like everyone else. He didn't believe what had really happened to me. He hadn't been there.

It was a reminder, though, that I couldn't share too much with Lois nor could I share any more with Will than I already had. As far as I could remember, anything I said could be taken as just someone bouncing ideas around. I was just a woman going back to confront her past, planning on returning to work afterwards because that was what people did.

I finished the day fuming at Anson. I snapped at Sandy when I took her some work and immediately apologized. She was gracious about it, realizing I was not at my best after having been the one to find Deborah.

"You'll feel better after we have her celebration of life. We'll have it at the conference center downstairs. She had some friends in the area but we decided that since Deborah didn't have a regular church, we'd just hold it there. It can hold all the people at the bank and we can offer our prayers there as well as anywhere," Sandy said. "She was a Unitarian and I've contacted that minister to speak."

"Thanks for doing this, Sandy." I was grateful someone was thinking about it because I was lost in my own little world. Deborah wasn't my favorite person. She annoyed me often, probably because she thought our mutual past in the Northwest should have made us instant friends, but she wasn't a bad person. She deserved to be remembered.

25

TRACI: SEPTEMBER NOW

The conference room that Deborah's service was held in was less like a typical conference room than it was an auditorium. The bank held company meetings in that space, so there was no question that there were plenty of places to sit.

A stage in the front held only a table behind which hung a large plain white wall to project images on. Today it was covered in images of Deborah, a few personal ones of her as a child, as well as adult ones, most from around Charlotte. Her friends in the area must have provided them. Flower arrangements decorated the room.

Seats were arranged on tiers going up and formed a horseshoe shape around the stage. Every seat had a good view, assuming you weren't too uncomfortable in them. None of the padded blue chairs leaned back very far and the aisles along which they were arranged were as narrow as the most crowded theater seating.

The overhead lights were dimmed, as they often were, giving the room a somber mood. I waited until it was nearly time to start before going in. I hadn't want to sit in the semi-dark for any longer than I had to.

I slipped into a seat in the second row on the right, sitting next to a young man in a suit that I didn't know at all. He glanced over at me and then turned to the front. I noticed Anson in the very back on the right. I didn't see Will. Nils was in the front row, nearly at the center. He'd just sat down when I slipped in.

A man in black robes walked onto the stage, appearing as if from nowhere, though I knew there was a space behind the white wall. Reaching the podium he began to talk about Deborah. I listened, trying to be polite, trying to learn about Deborah's life and maybe find any clues as to why she was chosen by Lucy. I wanted to know what Deborah could have done to attract the ghost, other than use a rest stop toilet, one that was used by millions who had never been murdered while they did their business. While I resembled many of the other murdered women, Deborah did not. I understood why Anson believed there wasn't any supernatural involvement. If I hadn't seen what I had in Steely Woods, I wouldn't believe it either.

I watched as pictures behind the minister changed. There was one of Deborah at a company picnic, something I'd actually gone to. I remembered the sunny day and how happy people were.

The next slide was of a grinning skull. I put my hand over my mouth, biting back a scream. No one else commented as the minister droned on. I turned to look around. Anson was looking to the side of the room, not at the screen. Nils, I noticed, stared at the image. He and Anson saw the skull, too. I was sure of it.

The next slide was black. I watched, thinking that my own haunting was over and that someone had just put in a poorly lit image. But no, in the background something lighter moved, appearing slowly like in a movie. In a moment, I made out a skeletal hand reaching towards the minister.

My heart began to pound and my hands began to sweat as I watched the arm come out of the image, a stray bit of skin, now gone brown from ages in the dirt clinging to the index finger. It brushed the back of the minister's head.

The minister rubbed his hand against the back of his head, like he was brushing off a fly.

I gasped, but it was a slight sound, and only the young man in the next chair looked over at me, frowning.

I didn't say anything, just bit down on my finger, wondering what to do. The hand had pulled back, avoiding the minister's hand wave. It reached out again but the slide changed.

This time Deborah's face smiled out at us from the screen.

I breathed out, realizing I'd been holding my breath. I hoped it didn't sound too much like a sigh. My thumbnail was bitten down practically to the finger.

I glanced around, looking at people. A couple had phones out, but most were paying attention to the minister. No one looked as horrified as I felt, though I didn't have a good view of many faces.

Someone coughed in the back and a few people shuffled feet. I got a whiff of a too-strong chemical rose scent of perfume. Probably the older woman on the other side of the young man. She'd just shifted in her seat. I wondered how he could breathe through the smell.

In a picture of Deborah sitting down at a group meeting of the marketing department, where I was sitting in the chair next to Nils, a dark figure hovered behind me. I stared. A couple of people gasped, the same sort of low gasp I had made earlier. This picture wasn't just my imagination.

I looked around. The young man stared back at me horrified.

The next slide came on and it appeared normal. The minister continued talking about Deborah's kindness to others and her interest in their well-being. If I hadn't been so horrified by the photos, something you expected in a horror movie, not real life, I'd have chuckled. What a grand way of saying she was nosey.

The minster wound down and called for a moment of silent reflection. He bowed his head. The screen went black behind him, this time because the slides of Deborah were over. I didn't close my eyes, though I bowed my head. The room went nearly silent except for the occasional brush of fabric against fabric as people fidgeted in their chairs.

I remained still. The comfort of the chairs, or lack of it, made no difference. I stared at the screen, my heart still beating rapidly, as I waited for a hand to come out and stroke the minister's hair. I kept staring at the dark screen, long after the minster finished the moment of silence and moved aside so that Nils could stand up and offer a few words about Deborah. Apparently, he'd talked to people in the office because he had a lot to say, telling a few favorite stories, which made me smile a little.

In one, Deborah had been brand new and she'd gotten off on the wrong floor on her second day. Arriving where her desk was supposed to be, she'd found Sonja sitting there. Instead of believing Sonja that she was on the wrong floor, Deborah had argued with her, thinking, for some reason, that this was some sort of horrible hazing ritual. Only when Sonja had called HR and asked what floor Deborah worked on did Deborah relent. By that time, she'd probably noticed that no one else looked at all familiar.

Even then, Nils said, she'd come down, looking around defensively as if she still wasn't certain she wasn't being toyed with. Deborah had even gone to his office and asked, just to be sure.

I remembered that. Sonja had talked about the incident for weeks. She couldn't believe anyone would think we'd be that mean to a new employee. Sonja was generally quiet, keeping to herself. She dressed formally and kept her hair cut very short, probably so she didn't have to mess with it every morning. Her deep brown, nearly black skin practically sparkled with health. The fact that she went on about this for some time was out of character and finally allowed many of us to get to know her a bit better than just a name and a familiar face.

Soon enough Nils finished speaking. No one else went up to talk. The lights came up and people stood, eager to get out of the uncomfortable chairs. A few went down and chatted with Nils. Other people talked and gossiped with each other. Pretty soon conversations swirled around the room making it hard to hear even one's own voice.

I slipped out of the room, not caring to talk to anyone. I saw Anson sitting in a chair, a hand partly covering his face, staring at the screen as if there was something to see. Maybe there was, at least to him. I didn't know. I was thankful the white screen looked blank to me.

I rode the elevator back to my nearly silent floor. I hurried down to my office, passing empty cubicles. We were Deborah's closest coworkers, so of course most people had remained in the conference room. Although being alone in such a large space bothered me, I reminded myself the lights were bright and my office had a window.

I slipped into my familiar zone and settled in front of my computer. As I moved the mouse around on my desk, planning to the get to work, the lights above my head went off and my computer died.

I swore softly. My heart pounded. After having just seen

the images on screen, I was in no mood to have to deal with the darkness. The blinds on my window were up, letting in light, but the day had gotten surprisingly overcast and what light there was remained muted gray.

Somewhere in the office, a faucet dripped. It wasn't the sound of a bathroom faucet drip, I reminded myself, sitting very still, moving my chair as close to the window as I could.

I pressed the side of my face against the cool window glass, picking up the faintest hint of citrus. I kept an eye on the office door. I considered closing it, but if something happened and I needed to get out, it would take me longer to flee.

I wished I had taken a moment to grab my cell phone, which sat just out of reach on a charger. Not only would it allow me to call for help, it had a flashlight app. But I needed to stay in the pool of gray light.

I heard papers being shuffled. I wondered if someone else had returned just after me or if the sound was of something moving in the depths of the office.

I drew in a breath. I thought I heard someone walking, the slight squeak of a rubber-soled shoe on carpet. I waited, staring at the door.

Who had on rubber-soled shoes? I couldn't think. More than likely, today, it was a man. Many women had dressed in skirts, perhaps wanting to look their best for the ceremony for Deborah. I had on a black skirt and a gray blouse with black and white pinstripes. It had a ruffle on the sleeve making it more festive than I would have liked, but it was the only sort of black thing I had.

No one came by my door.

I hated waiting. My muscles remained tense, protesting against remaining frozen by the window. They'd been held in one position too often for too long recently not to start protesting quickly.

I wished the lights would come on.

The air conditioning kicked in with a clunk and I jumped. The air flowed over my head, lifting my hair and I was reminded of the minister brushing away the skeletal hand.

The hairs on the back of my neck prickled. My stomach knotted.

I tried to tell myself this was normal from the air conditioning and that I had nothing to fear.

I heard a clank and scratching coming from the air conditioning vent. I was again reminded of the skeletal presence I had seen dragging itself through the image on the screen.

The sound repeated.

Pause.

Repeat.

Whatever was up there was getting louder. Closer.

My breath hitched.

My chest felt too tight to take in a breath. I didn't dare. I shook all over.

How much more of this could I take? I had thought I was doing something. Now this.

"Why?" I whispered.

I felt this rush of anger, as if I were standing in front of the angriest person I knew and hearing them vent, feeling the fear that they were going to hit me or lash out with something even worse than a fist. The physical sensation of that anger and fear made me cringe.

The sounds coming from the air conditioner stopped, as did the air.

I heard nothing.

There was the faintest smell of spoiled milk and then that too was gone.

The lights came up.

My chest loosened enough so I could breathe, though I

didn't draw as much air in as I'd like. I was still alone. Could still be harmed.

The elevator dinged.

I held onto the window sill where I was crouched to keep myself from running out into the hallway to meet whoever was on the elevator.

I imagined running towards the sound only to find a skeletal figure coming out, grinning back at me, the lights darkening around me.

Instead of moving, I listened to voices murmuring, felt the slight tremble of the floors as a dozen or so people walked out of the elevator, heading to cubicles and offices.

Now I could let in all the air I needed. Now I could focus on calming my heart.

I glanced up at the air vent. It was just over my desk. Usually I liked that. Now, it worried me. I pictured an arm snaking down behind me as I tried to work.

I remained by the window, biting my lip, trying to decide what to do.

Before I'd begun to think about facing my fears they had been limited in scope. Yes, bathrooms were important and I couldn't avoid them. Yes, darkness was hard to avoid but I'd managed it and still had some sort of life, though most would say it was a dull existence.

Now, though, now… Now everything in my life was up for grabs. A meeting hall surrounded by people, my office, my office chair, places I hadn't worried about before.

I tried to get up to leave. I leaned against the wall to help but even that wasn't enough. I slid down and wrapped my arms around myself, head down on my knees, not caring how I looked. After all, I had an excuse that day didn't I?

I stayed that way until Will found me.

LUCY: EARLY FALL THEN

The wind made it feel colder than it was and even the tall trees didn't stop the breeze from cutting through Lucy's thin jacket. If she'd had a heavier coat, she'd have worn it, but coats cost money that Alma said they didn't have. Lucy put on a second shirt from her pillow-case and hurried through the woods, hoping that movement would keep her warmer.

The wind rattled the branches of the trees together making enough of a racket that if someone were following her, Lucy wouldn't know. Now and then birds would titter to each other and that would make her feel calmer. Surely if there was someone else there, the birds would go silent.

The whole woods smelled of pine. There was a hint of rain in the air too, that damp scent that said darker clouds were coming, heavy with water. Lucy shivered in anticipation. If she could smell the rain, it wasn't far off and she'd be soaked before she made town.

She could hurry to school but Lucy wasn't sure she trusted the people there. Alma may have made an excuse for her and someone could call her and tell her Lucy had arrived for lessons.

No, she had to keep moving. It would make sense to try and grab a ride from the freeway but instead she headed towards the main road through town. If men she did know, had known since she was a baby, couldn't wait to put their sweaty hands on her naked body, Lucy worried that strangers would do even more horrible things, though her mind could conjure no images of anything worse than what had gone before.

Lucy hoped to run into Mrs. Pinterstock heading to the post office. Maybe someone in the larger town would be going to Olympia or Portland and she could get ride with them. She had to stay hidden until she saw the right car, though. It wouldn't do to let Alma see her. She had no idea what her sister might do.

Lucy rubbed her nose with her cold fingers as she sniffled. She wouldn't cry. How had this sister who she had loved come to be someone who would lock her in the trailer so Lucy couldn't even go to school? It was like Alma was trying to destroy her.

Lucy would never do that to a younger sister if she had one. If she were the oldest, she'd have told the men to jump in a lake and found a real job. Maybe she'd have moved them far away and into a city where she could find a job that would pay for a room for a couple of young women.

It would have been better for both of them, but Alma had been too scared and had insisted upon staying around, trying to live on handouts from creeps. If Alma had made better decisions, she would have seen that letting Lucy finish school and get a good job, as a secretary or even a nurse, would have helped both of them.

But no. Alma made her decision and when she had gotten

tired of that life, she foisted it off on her sister. Except Alma worked Lucy harder than she had ever worked herself. It had only been on Sundays that Alma had had a man in her bed, a man who allowed her to keep her job and the crummy trailer. She expected Lucy to spend just about every night of the week with a man, each one different and horrible in his own way. And when those men paid, they gave their cash to Alma, not Lucy.

No more.

The trees thinned and the small township came into view. It was a sad place really, just a single road with the gas station, the café, and general store. A small sheriff's station was around the corner, as if by hiding it, the sheriff could catch more criminals. The fire department was up the road a few miles, near the post office, the hotel, and the grocery store. You could get most things at the general store, but groceries were cheaper if you could get over there.

Out of the trees, the wind whipped harder. Lucy had to plant her feet to keep from being pushed forward. It was going to be quite a storm. If Alma saw her, it would probably frighten her into thinking the trailer had been smashed. That would serve her right.

Of course, with such a storm, Mrs. Pinterstock probably wasn't going to the post office.

Lucy waited near the edge of the trees, watching the road. No cars went past. She continued to wait, standing still, watching. The wind howled under the eaves of the café and rattled branches. Rain fell. It wasn't a hard rain, just an easy, steady mist that made it hard to see.

A big black pickup cruised down the road. Not Mrs. Pinterstock. Lucy didn't go running out, although she was cold enough that she considered it.

The café door banged open and Alma marched out. She turned back to someone and swore at them. She tossed aside her apron and stomped across the street. Something had displeased her. Lucy slipped back into the woods, hoping her sister wouldn't see her. She huddled off the path, sinking down into a crouch but not willing to crawl under a bush because of how wet it was.

"Asshole," Alma was snarling. "I'll get him a treat. A girl treat. Goddamn it, Lucy better not fight me on this. I am so not in the mood."

Lucy listened to the rant for as long as she was able, holding her position and trying not to give away where she was. She wasn't worried about sound, but worried Alma might catch a hint of her movements and be tempted to look closer.

She needn't have worried. All the trees and bushes swayed and rattled in the wind. An army could have been crouched down in hiding and a single walker would have been none the wiser.

Lucy hurried out to the road after her sister disappeared. She walked along the street, not staying too close. She regretted letting the truck go by. She needed a ride out of town. She'd stay on the road for as long as she could and then duck into the fields or the woods if it got too late. Alma might not have a car but that didn't mean she couldn't persuade someone else to go after Lucy.

Lucy didn't know exactly who needed a treat but she figured it was Clyde at the café. Maybe he wanted Alma instead of Lucy and Alma was having none of it.

The rain started to fall harder. Lucy moved over to the tree line, hoping she'd remain drier. She couldn't tell that it helped much, her coat and shirts were soaked through, water dripping down her bare skin beneath the layers.

The rain made her even colder, and Lucy shivered so hard her teeth clicked together each time the wind tore through her thin clothing. Lucy was so miserable she didn't hear the car drive by. Mrs. Pinterstock had gone out that day in her lovely sedan, which Lucy had longed to see. She ran to the road and waved her arms but Mrs. Pinterstock wasn't looking at the rearview mirror.

Lucy groaned. Tears threatened. Of all the days for Alma to decide she needed to be locked in, forcing her to make the decision, it had to be on such a miserable one.

Feeling sorry for herself, Lucy didn't hear the growl of the truck behind her until it was on her, stopping beside her.

"Need a ride?" It was the bearded man. Lucy had long since learned he went by Will but she never thought of him like that. If he had a name, she had to consider that he might actually be human. Bearded Man made him a thing. It kept him equal to her.

"I'm just walking," Lucy said.

"Get in," he ordered.

Lucy shook her head and walked further into the trees, hoping he wouldn't get out.

She breathed a sigh of relief when he drove on.

It wasn't too long after that she heard the growl of another truck but she stayed near the trees, hoping the driver would ignore her. She was getting close to the town, the real town, where there was a post office and a city hall and a real grocery store, not their little township that held so little.

The truck stopped and Lucy's stomach dropped. She looked over.

Alma was hopping out and running towards her.

Lucy bolted for the trees. She couldn't be caught. Not now.

Normally, Lucy was faster, but she was tired and wet. Alma was angry, the rage still carving her face into a parody of the lovely young woman she'd once been.

Both women ran for their lives, but for different reasons.

Lucy made it to the edge of town, crossing the backyard of a family. A red metal swing and a plastic tub for wading indicated children lived there. Lucy took note of those things, wondering if she should detour to bang on the door, when Alma grabbed her coat.

Lucy struggled but Alma's grip was strong. Stronger than Lucy would have thought.

"You can't run, you stupid little bitch. I am not filling in for you," Alma snarled.

"I am not your property," Lucy screamed. She hoped that someone was home. Maybe the mother of those children. Maybe she'd come out and ask what was going on. But no one appeared.

Alma started dragging Lucy along. The truck she had come in had followed their path but stayed on the road. Closer, Lucy saw the bearded man waiting, smiling in the cab.

"Quite a workout you had there, Little Lucy."

Alma was trying to push her into the cab.

Lucy spit at Will.

He wiped the spit from his beard and glared at her, eyes hard.

It was only then that Lucy realized she'd made a horrible mistake.

"How much do I pay to address this particular insult?" he asked Alma.

"How long she gonna be out of work?" Alma asked, pragmatically. Lucy could hear the edge in her sister's voice that said she was mad, but Lucy had no illusions that the anger was at the bearded man. Alma was mad at her.

"Long time," the man said.

Alma sighed, pushing Lucy in the truck. She didn't immediately name a number.

27

TRACI: SEPTEMBER NOW

I preferred to travel by plane, as I felt safer in the air. It doesn't seem like the kind of place a ghost would attack. Plus, planes were always crowded, and the life around me helped keep the spirits at bay.

I'd had to make reservations late, which meant I'd purchased a first class ticket. I had aisle seats on both legs, the first to Phoenix and the second to Portland, which seemed like an odd way to go, but apparently, that was the easiest way to get there.

I appreciated the comfortable seat which let me spread out and stretch my legs. In the plane I was surrounded by people which allowed me to relax a little. The noise of the engines kept me from hearing any strange sounds, like the drip of a faucet. First class smelled faintly of vodka and bacon. This was the early flight.

After eating a bit, I settled back to sleep. I'd brought a kindle to read, but I was yawning before the plane took off. I couldn't remember the last time I'd felt so relaxed. While I didn't know for certain that my ghost wouldn't appear on the plane, I did know it tended to avoid crowded places. I avoided thinking about the moment it had reached a hand out to the minister talking about Deborah, though I thought only Anson, Nils, and I saw the hand. The noise and the movement as well as the fact that the plane flew above any clouds into a bright and sunny sky, all made me feel more comfortable.

If I could have lived on a plane, I would have. It felt that safe.

The sun shone brightly in Phoenix and I found a warm window to wait next to. I used the restroom shortly before landing and was able to avoid the public bathroom at the airport. I avoided drinking too many fluids. I was antsier at the airport, as if being closer to Lucy made my fears stronger. Still, there were plenty of people around. Noise cascaded over me, the beeps of moving vehicles, the sounds of people talking, and the intercom announcing flights and boarding kept me from hearing anything I shouldn't.

Arriving in Portland was hard. The familiar blue carpet that looked like someone had dropped pink confetti on it gave me a chill. The cloudy day made the terminal feel too dark, despite the lights. I had only my carry-on. I would have to purchase an electric lantern along with my other paraphernalia after leaving the airport. Fortunately, Portland was home, and I knew where I could shop.

Years had changed the place. Instead of driving down a road to get to I-205, looking at low trees and bushes, I was met with a large strip mall on the inland side that included a Best Buy and an Ikea. There were more cars than I remembered, and I struggled to stay with traffic. I'd booked a Best Western in Vancouver across the river in Washington because it had had the lowest price.

It was only four but I got stuck in traffic crossing the I-205 bridge. If I remembered correctly there was a Fred Meyer just off the Mill Plain exit. I'd stopped there often when I was going up to see Ronette. It was the place I'd normally pick up my Diet Coke and any snacks before heading back on the road to visit my friend. I wondered how much the store had changed.

The Mill Plain exit came up faster than expected and I almost missed the turn off. Someone behind me honked, reminding me that this was no longer my home.

I hadn't set a radio station. Everything about the little Kia was different from my own car. I drove quickly while trying to get used to the unfamiliar layout. I hoped I'd signaled before going over. Of course, if the person behind me had wanted to be mad, they'd be mad no matter what.

Rain started to fall, that light rain that was just hard enough that you couldn't see out the windshield, but doesn't wet the glass enough to allow the windshield wipers to work smoothly. The Kia's squeaked and squawked at me as I drove. I found the Fred Meyer and drove around the parking lot looking for a space. The store seemed busier than it used too, or maybe I just wasn't used to being there at right around rush hour.

I finally found a spot as a woman in a Subaru pulled out. I parked and hurried inside, trying to cover my head. The evening was darker than I had thought it would be. While I had expected it to be darker than Charlotte, knowing the Pacific Northwest was rarely without at least a few clouds, I had forgotten how much further north the area was. We were going into fall. The sun was already starting to sink below the horizon.

At least it wasn't full dark just yet. Unfortunately, there was a good chance it would be before I got to the hotel, especially if I stopped for a meal. I sighed. There was no help for it now. In Charlotte, even at this hour, it would still be full light.

I hurried through my shopping, thankful for the people

that I had to push around and the woman who bumped into me. I hovered over apples that smelled heavenly. I used to take that smell for granted. There were apples in Charlotte, but they weren't these apples that looked and smelled so perfect, almost glowing with nutrition that they were dying to offer.

I couldn't help myself and purchased some, though I didn't really need food. I got two electric lanterns, an extra flashlight, plenty of batteries, candles, incense, salt, garlic, and paper. I'd found a sage bundle for clearing at Whole Foods before I left. I considered more food besides the apples and picked up some candy as well as some crackers and cheese. I could easily fix that for myself as a snack if I were hungry later on.

I packed up my purchases and headed up the highway to the hotel. It was nearly full dark now. I suspected if it wasn't so cloudy there would have been light on the horizon, a pink band leaving me hope of getting somewhere before full dark. Unfortunately, I'd hit a cloudy afternoon. I shouldn't have expected anything else. Charlotte had spoiled me.

I was lucky to get a spot in front of the Best Western. The lights around the parking lot were all on, shining down on the entry. I grabbed my small suitcase and the bag carrying the electric lanterns and went in.

The place looked cheery and fairly new. I didn't have much reason to go to Vancouver when I'd lived there, only passing through it, stopping at the Fred Meyer for things to fortify me for a drive north. I didn't know if the hotel really was new or if I just hadn't seen it before.

The lobby smelled of fresh pine and vanilla. The floors were designed to absorb the sounds of people walking. Low blue carpet lined the main lounge area where a gas fireplace was lit, the flames leaving dancing shadows against the walls.

My neck crawled. Moving shadows made it harder to pin point those that were unnatural.

Fortunately, there wasn't a wait to get checked in, so I didn't need to stay in the lobby very long. I headed up to my room on the second floor. Getting off the tiny, but bright elevator, I was thankful that the hallway was both wide and well-lit. I heard a television from a room across the hall. In another, I heard someone talking, probably on the phone as I heard only one voice.

My key worked easily and I opened the door onto darkness. I reached in to turn on a light. My hand felt cold. The lights came on and I saw nothing strange. I breathed out.

I stepped in, turning on the bathroom light, not looking in there, not wanting to see what might lurk in the dark. I'd seen things in the light, but for some reason the light made me feel safer. When everything was on, I set around my electric lanterns. I found the heat and turned it up. The room was cold, but someone had set the temperature down lower than my thin North Carolina blood was comfortable with.

I closed the drapes so I didn't have to look out onto the dark trees that lined the path behind the hotel. I was on the quiet side, but that meant my view was of trees and the tops of other buildings, a perfect place for something to go sliding around. Other people might love it, but I found it frightening.

Having set things up, I went out to grab the rest of my stuff. I was going to have to rest up for my drive the next day. I was meeting Lois at noon the next day which meant I'd need to be up early. As Washington was three hours behind Charlotte that shouldn't be a problem. Ronette was going to meet me at a Burger King which was just off the highway where I'd need to turn around.

She'd waited until nearly the last minute to get back to

me, but she'd come through. I didn't know how I'd ever repay her.

Once I bought everything into the room, I tried to settle in. I couldn't concentrate to read and I hated the way the television made me feel as if I were in my own little world, unable to hear people moving around in the hotel or talking in their rooms. Once, I thought I heard the single drip of a faucet. I listened harder, but heard only the sounds of someone in another room turning on the shower.

Perhaps I was safe there. Perhaps not.

Despite my extra lights, the hotel felt dark. It hadn't when I'd come in, but as time passed, the room felt as if it were closing in, getting darker the smaller it got, the tiny space eating away at the light. I knew it had to be my imagination.

I thought about Anson's comments. Our minds search for ways to make things make sense. The room wasn't darker, or if it was, perhaps as the night settled in whatever light from the outside had dimmed leaving the room less bright. Or maybe it was all in my head and as I sat there I noticed how dark the room really was. Maybe whatever had happened to me at the rest stop had caused me to go crazy and I couldn't even trust my eyes to notice whether a hotel room was actually dark or not.

I didn't believe I was crazy, but wasn't it a sign of mental illness to be certain of your sanity?

The last meal I had had was on the plane. I looked at the apples I purchased at Fred Meyer. Two of them. Both were red striated with pink and they smelled so heavenly, but my stomach was too knotted for me to be hungry.

Maybe in the morning or maybe later I'd want to eat.

I had slept on the plane, but that brief rest had not been nearly enough. Although the bed was comfortable, I had a feeling my mind wasn't going to let me rest very well in the hotel.

I looked in the bathroom, gauging the light. Did I dare take a shower?

The light flickered just a little. The heat lamp made a long buzzing sound. I worried that the light would burn itself out before I could finish washing my hair and body. I couldn't shower in there, not at night.

I sighed. Maybe after I found Lucy I'd feel better.

I lay down and tried to sleep.

28

TRACI: SEPTEMBER NOW

Morning rolled around and I was up before dawn had cleared the horizon. I needed to shower and I did so, quickly. The lights stayed on and nothing crawled into the shower with me. I used the hotel shampoo so both I and the bathroom smelled of citrus and spice. It was an uplifting scent.

The smell wasn't enough to keep me from feeling shaky and uncertain but it was enough that I didn't feel quite as terrified as I had been.

I ate an apple and packed up my things. I had a reservation for the next night but I didn't know if I'd need it. I wanted to have everything I brought with me because I had no idea what I'd need when I was at the rest stop.

Originally, I had planned to just do some daylight reconnaissance. I'd go back on the next night to do the ceremony, but now I was hoping to have it all done in one day. That way, I'd have more time to visit with Ronette, assuming all went well.

Other people in the hotel were up early as well, and I was surrounded by the sounds of running water, low voices talking, and the squeak and groan of the floors. I heard the faint ding of the elevator bell when it arrived on my floor. I gathered my things and headed out. I considered eating something more at the complimentary breakfast, but I decided to wait. If I had to go to the bathroom on the drive, it would give me an excuse to stop at a Starbucks. Most of their stores, the ones I was familiar with, had single stall bathrooms and if I had to use a public bathroom, I felt safer in those.

I wouldn't get coffee even if I needed the caffeine. Caffeine might make me have to use the restroom sooner than I wanted. Instead, I'd get a scone and a small bottle of water.

I got in my little Kia which smelled faintly of a spicy cologne, perhaps from the last user. I readjusted the seat, trying to get it right. Then I looked through the manual and checked that I knew where the turn signal was, the headlights, the gas-cap door. I started up and began to wend my way north.

I was going to be early to the Burger King if I made good time. At least Ronette wouldn't be left waiting there, wondering what had happened. She couldn't say I stood her up if I were early.

The day had dawned clearer than the day before, but it wasn't without clouds. Still, plenty of pink sky peeked out between the gray and white puff-ball clouds and it looked as if more clouds were drifting away than in.

Traffic wasn't too bad going north at that time of day. It wasn't completely clear sailing, but I was thankful to be moving in the direction I was. Southbound was clearly another matter, the lanes packed with cars and many coming to a complete stop for several minutes.

I was both comforted by the evergreens that lined the freeway and disconcerted at being back. My heart pounded and my mouth went dry thinking about the last time I'd traveled I-5. Another part of me was overcome with shock at how much had changed—it used to be a long way out to Ridgefield but now the entire drive from Vancouver to Ridgefield was completely built up, and that building even included an amphitheater.

Nearly twenty years was a long time to be gone. It was shocking to see the changes, but I suppose it shouldn't have been. I'd read a lot about how everyone loved Portland. Articles like that always made me a little homesick, although I always sort of wished that all those people singing the praises of Portland had experienced what I'd experienced. Maybe they wouldn't be so thrilled with the Northwest after all.

Traffic slowed a little near the Kelso/Longview area but then it picked back up again. I was at the Burger King with over an hour to go. I sighed, sitting in the little car. I wasn't hungry, at least not then, and I didn't know when Ronette would get there. She didn't have quite as far to travel as I did, but perhaps there was more traffic for her.

I checked for text messages. There was one from Will wishing me well. I sent him a quick note back.

There was another, from earlier, about the time I had set out from an unknown number. I figured that it was probably just an advertiser or perhaps someone with a wrong number.

"Looking forward to meeting you."

My first thought was Lois, but we'd not exchanged phone numbers. A chill went down my back, long and hard enough that I was close to turning around and leaving, not just the Burger King, but the Northwest. I entertained the fantasy of moving to England. Our bank had a partner bank over there. Then I thought of the long cloudy days and old buildings with faucets that probably dripped on a regular basis and knew I could never survive there.

Either Lois had found my phone number because she was a good researcher or it was something else.

I couldn't have said which was worse.

My mouth felt dry. My hands shook. I didn't want to be alone any longer. There were two cars going through the drive-thru and one parked in front of the restaurant. I got out and went in. At least there, people would be serving, even if the other customer finished and left.

Although I wasn't particularly hungry or thirsty, I ordered a Dr. Pepper. I'd given up Diet Coke the night I'd nearly died. I hadn't wanted to, but my stomach had heaved at the idea every time I'd tried to drink it and I'd gradually decided that particular soda was another casualty of the night I had nearly died.

I didn't order lunch. It was too early. I'd missed their breakfast hours. I did get some French fries to nibble on and hopefully keep them from asking me to leave because I hadn't purchased enough.

I sat at one of the tables near a window, the side where the sun was coming in. Behind the counter that separated the kitchen from the eating area, shadows moved and length-ened. Sometimes I thought I saw a hand reaching out to me.

I shook my head and looked down at my phone. I nibbled my fries and played a game. Time ticked by.

I logged onto the Cold Case Forum to see if Lois had posted anything. She'd sent a message similar to the one I had gotten by text.

"I'm setting off. Looking forward to meeting you. Who knows what we'll find?"

She seemed a little too cheery for what we were doing. Given the time, I had a feeling she'd be early. Maybe she'd find Lucy's remains before I even got there. I was starting to think this was a ridiculous idea, but it was the only one I had.

I nibbled a few more fries.

I sipped the Dr. Pepper. I'd never much liked it before I moved south and it was everywhere. Now it was my soda of choice. I hadn't quite gotten into sweet tea. Maybe it was a taste you had to be born with.

A car backfired and made me jump, reminding me of exactly how tense I was. I tried to concentrate on my breathing but it didn't help. If anything, doing so made things worse. I was probably getting used to the fact that I only concentrated on breathing when I was terrified. Perhaps my body was responding accordingly.

I ought to look into more therapy when I got home. I clearly needed more help than I was getting.

I ate another fry.

I was about to start another game of solitaire when I saw a heavy set woman with purple hair getting out of her car. It was a short curly bob, just like Ronette had always worn her hair. When she stood up and turned, I knew it was her. She'd gotten rounder but there was also an air of confidence about her carriage that had been missing twenty years ago. Of course, raising a family had probably given her plenty of challenges to overcome.

She was dressed in jeans and a long-sleeved Henley knit pullover in pink. She pulled out her phone from a nicely designed beige and brown leather bag and looked at it. She didn't text.

I held my breath. She walked in and looked around, breaking into a smile when she saw me. I stood up, though my legs were shaky. I hadn't seen her in years. I'd forced myself to her wedding, but that was the last time. I'd nearly had a heart attack in the church bathrooms which had white stalls and a faucet that had dripped constantly.

I'd been near to losing it before we got to the hotel for the reception and I'd made a beeline for the room I was in. Even then, I'd been haunted by the sound of the faucet dripping made worse by the hotel room's dim lighting. I had gone in anyway and used the toilet. While I was in there, toilet paper had wrapped itself around my hands as if the unseen creature was trussing me up like a wedding gift.

I'd whimpered and groaned, pulling them apart, surprised when the toilet paper had broken with little effort. I had hurried out as fast as my rubbery legs could take me and stayed until I was the last one there, not because I was partying and having fun, but because I wasn't sure I could go back to my hotel room.

"Traci!" Ronette said, holding her arms out for a hug. Her voice was lower than I remembered but still held a sing song tone whenever she spoke.

I smiled and held my arms out. "It's good to see you," I said. "I'm so glad you were willing to come with me."

"No one knows how much the rest stop incident changed you more than me and maybe Dave," Ronette said, referring to my then-boyfriend.

I couldn't say anything.

Ronette let go of the hug and pushed me back a little, taking a long look at me. "It's not your fault. You must have been terrified. I know you tried to keep that all in and just push through but some things can't be pushed through. And clearly you're seeing you can't just run from them either."

My eyes got all teary and I tried not to choke on the sobs that started to fill my throat. When had my once best friend gotten so wise? And, I thought, so kind, given that we hadn't really talked in years, perhaps decades.

Ronette, seeing my reaction pulled me into another hug. "We'll talk when you're ready," she said. Then she sat and start prattling on about her children, as if we'd had lunch at Burger King every week for years. She nibbled on my fries and then got up and got herself a Whopper Junior. She got me an original chicken sandwich with cheese, just the way I had liked it.

I was getting myself back together when she brought the tray back to the table.

"So?" she said. "Tell me what brought you back and pushed you into checking into this. It can't be the other woman getting killed. A woman was killed not long after you had your scare and this has been over nineteen years. I remember it to the day because this all started the day after my birthday."

"One of my coworkers was killed in a rest stop in Charlotte," I said quietly.

"No shit?" Ronette paused in opening the wrapper around her burger.

I nodded. I hadn't touched my chicken sandwich, wasn't sure if I could eat while having that discussion.

"And you think this was about you?" Ronette pushed.

"I don't know," I said. "I mean the main reason I went so far away was to get away from whatever happened, but I see shadows and jump. I can't sleep without all the lights on. I can't use a public restroom unless I know it's private—no stalls. A dripping faucet sends me into a panic attack." I was getting choked up.

Ronette reached over and held my hand. "It's okay. We're here now and you're doing something."

"I read about the death here too," I said. "I think that's what started it. Deborah—the woman who died?—she was really fascinated by the deaths at Steely Woods. It's almost like it was connected even though I know that's crazy."

"Maybe it isn't crazy," Ronette said. I'd never told her what I really thought happened, about the fact that the hand I saw didn't just look skeletal but was bone and rotten flesh. I'd only told her about my terror and about the fact that two girls had come in and I'd been saved. She'd never pressed for specific details.

I waited. I quietly opened my chicken sandwich.

"I mean, that was a weird thing that happened. I've been following this last death a bit in the papers because I remembered the weekend you were there another woman died." Ronette paused and took a bite of her Whopper Junior. "It's weird. There's stuff on the internet claiming there has to be a cover-up because of the way things happened. I mean there's speculation that it's some sort of cult keeping a demon at bay with a sacrifice every twenty years. There's another that it's a police officer or trucker who kills women on a schedule. They've got a few other places where deaths have happened in the area, but I'm not sure how they link those. There are other people who think it's supernatural."

"Why?" I asked. I picked up my sandwich, wondering about taking a bite. I didn't look at Ronette, afraid that she might see the hope in my eyes that I was being validated.

"Because people have seen things for the last several weeks. Women who go into the restroom alone and think they hear something or see something. One woman started screaming and her husband came running in. The woman who died was alone. Her mom left to go out to the car earlier and it was only five minutes later that she went in and found her daughter. There were truckers across the way, but no one saw anything."

I nodded. "That's kind of what happened to Deborah."

"See? That's what makes people think it was supernatural. Otherwise, how did the killer leave?"

"Anson says that we use the supernatural to make sense out of things that don't make sense. Like this death."

"Anson is full of it," Ronette said. She took a big bite out of her burger, chewing quickly. She took a long drink of her soda, watching me the whole time.

"Maybe that's why I have stuff," I said. "To try and banish her. Or maybe just banish her from me."

"The girl that you're going searching for. With the woman with the dog?"

I nodded.

Ronette nodded as she ate. "Even if you aren't actually being haunted, if it's not about her, I think this will make you feel better. It's important. You've been letting the incident haunt you all this time. If there is a ghost, then you've been haunted twice, don't you see? Once from the ghost and once from your memories of this."

It was an interesting take. A little like Anson's but more like Anson's and mine together rather than an either or.

"A guy at worked talked like that, a little. But then when I started doing something about it, he kept on about how it couldn't be a ghost because they didn't exist. He was really adamant. I guess he felt like he was influencing me to go to do something stupid." I watched Ronette for her reaction.

"He's an idiot." She took a bit of food and chewed before continuing. "It doesn't matter what he thinks. He hasn't experienced what you have…"

"He was at the rest stop in North Carolina when Deborah was murdered," I interrupted.

"I don't care. He didn't see what you saw. He can't say whether you made up something to explain some bizarre thing or if you actually saw a ghost or a demon or something we don't have a name for. He can't. He might explain things his way and that's his comfort. You have to find your truth. I'll believe you no matter what."

"Thanks." I couldn't believe how supportive Ronette was being.

"You shut me out all those years ago," Ronette said. "I don't want you to do it again. I know we live on other sides of the country now, but that doesn't mean we can't stay close. We were once."

I wanted to deny that I had shut her out but looking back

she was probably right. I was so scared of everything, I couldn't even talk about the experience. I had tried but I was scared not only of repeating what I had seen, perhaps making it real, but of what people would think if I had told them.

I was haunted in more ways than Ronette knew.

TRACI: SEPTEMBER NOW

We took Ronette's car to the rest stop. I'd been attacked at the rest stop on the south side of the freeway so when we left the rest stop, we'd have to drive to the next exit and turn around. Ronette would take the exit with the Burger King and drop me off at my car. If all went well, I'd see her again in a couple of days, at least for a short visit. If things didn't go well, it probably didn't matter.

Ronette drove a blue Prius. I settled into the comfortable seats, smelling the slight scent of Chinese food, probably something Ronette picked up to eat far too often. It also smelled like her, that indefinable smell that I remembered from living with her in the dorm room. It was a tidy car, a small trash bag hanging on the side, one of those things you could purchase through the internet for the person who had everything. There wasn't any trash in it.

There were no extra napkins around. Two cloth shopping bags were folded neatly in the backseat on the driver's side. No crumbs dotted the floor or seats and the dash was suspiciously free of any dust. Her daughters were both in high school, but teenagers could be messy, although I wasn't surprised that Ronette's girls weren't. She'd been good about tidying up, though not quite obsessively. It occurred to me at some point that perhaps the car was as neat as it was because she hadn't seen me in so long and she wanted to put on a good face.

We talked about easy things as we drove back the way I had come. I watched the trees. The sun remained high in the sky. The clouds seemed a little heavier but they hadn't completely crowded out the blue beyond. From the looks of the sky, it would be clear when we met Lois.

It seemed like a good omen and I wanted to take good omens where I could.

We passed a semi-truck and Ronette pulled over into the right hand lane. A few minutes later I saw the blue sign for the rest area. Our conversation fell silent.

The trees whipped past even as we slowed down to take the exit.

In this particular rest area, semis went to the first parking lot and the cars to the second. The buildings had been placed in the middle. Two buildings housing restrooms framed a smallish middle area where volunteers often offered coffee and cookies. Two men sat at the table that day, both older men, the lines on their faces attesting to their age. They laughed easily and whatever bad had happened, I knew they'd not just survived as I was doing, they actually lived.

Several cars were parked in the car lot and a man and woman sat eating sandwiches at a picnic table over to one side, beneath several large trees. Across the way, a tall young woman dressed in jeans and a hooded sweatshirt emblazoned with WSU walked a German Shepherd. She didn't look at us as she watched where she walked.

"That's not her is it?" Ronette asked.

I didn't answer right away, looking at the evergreen trees

interspersed with broad leafed trees that lined the far side of the lot. I remembered that night, the night everything began, when their branches had appeared to reach out to me, echoing the skeletal fingers that had reached for me in the bathroom.

"No," I said, finally. "Lois has a standard poodle."

Ronette and I got out of the car. It felt good to stretch, though I didn't like being there. I wasn't terrified the way I had expected. I just felt dread, the way you do when you know you have to have a root canal and don't want to. It was almost as if by getting here, I just wanted things to be over and done with so I could get on about my life.

Ronette looked at her phone. "It's not even noon yet," she said. "We both made really good time."

We had and for that I was grateful. Without a word we both wandered towards the dog walking area. It was a large grassy area with trees beyond. I smelled the scent of evergreen cedars and firs and noted the thin birches that were often used as a windbreak, so different from trees in the south. It was cooler than I was used to, and even with my jacket I felt chilly. The sun didn't seem as warm in this part of the world. It had been foolish of me to expect it to considering how much further north I was.

A sidewalk separated the field from the parking lot and Ronette and I walked along it. We reached the end, as the parking area became an off ramp and then turned to go back the other way. I saw a green Forester drive into the parking lot and find a space facing the dog park. A black poodle raised its head in the backseat.

"I bet that's them," I said.

A gray-haired man got out. He wore a jacket in dark blue that hung on him as if it were a size too large. He was average height, and while on the thin side, he wasn't skinny. He wore khaki trousers and tennis shoes. The woman who came around from the passenger side looked like the picture Lois had sent me so that I'd recognize her. She was taller than I had expected, almost half a head taller than the man.

She looked spryer than he did, in jeans, albeit elastic-waist jeans, tennis shoes, and a red fleece jacket. She moved with an ease he lacked. I guessed he had arthritis in his back or hips and perhaps his shoulders as well. He took care with movements. She took them for granted.

Together they leashed up the poodle which leaped out but didn't go running off. It did raise its head and began sniffing the air. It pranced around looking at both of its owners as if asking what was next, making sure they knew it was ready for adventure. Lois held the dog while her husband slammed the door and locked it.

They looked around, as if uncertain what to do next.

Ronette and I hurried over.

Introductions went easily. Lois' husband was named Scott. I introduced Ronette by her first name only. If this was a scam of some sort, no need to give them any more information than necessary. We probably should have taken the rental car. That way a license plate search wouldn't lead them back to Ronette. However, I had a feeling these two were on the up and up, unless Scott was the one who had killed Lucy all those years ago. Mentally doing the math, I realized that he was too young to have been involved, even if he did look old.

"Let's go that way." Lois pointed off to the south and west. "I was researching and I think that area is more likely to be unused. The body they found when they were building this particular rest area was under the south building and I'd think that they'd have found something closer if there were more. I want to start on this side, by the trees. That wouldn't have been as explored."

Scott had little to say, as if he wasn't sure about this. He had the look of a man who was used to giving into what he probably thought of as his wife's whims. He followed along with her and the dog, shuffling a little now and then. Fortunately, the dog, Mercedes didn't hurry. Lois told her to search and she got right down to it. I was impressed.

Mercedes led us into the treed area. It wasn't a woods, exactly but more a tamed wooded land that extended back further than I could measure, not that I was good at eyeballing distances. There were plenty of trees and some low ferns growing near the ground along with a greenish yellow ground cover. Few small bushes and no fallen trees marred our trek. I was reminded of the areas just off the paths of most Northwest hiking trails. Clearer than virgin forest but not totally clear, merely tamed a little.

Mercedes sniffed around the trees and ferns. A squirrel charged through the ferns and scampered up a tree, distracting her, but only for a few moments. I thought I saw a look of longing on the dog's face but it disappeared quickly and she got back to work.

When we were a few yards into the woods, they got less tamed and darker. The pine and cedar branches formed a tighter mesh overhead so the sun didn't peak through quite as much. Looking up, the clouds had come in, though they didn't seem like they would bring rain. A cold breeze filtered through the leaves and branches. I noticed Scott shiver a little.

Shadows moved with the breeze and mentally I had to make sure all of them belonged to a tree or bush. There were some I couldn't account for, but I also couldn't account for every branch at that angle of the sun. Still, I felt unsettled. My stomach tied itself in knots. I wanted this to be over.

Mercedes continued on, unaffected by the breeze and the clouds. Her tail was up and it twitched now and then before going straight and still. She was all business. Lois kept her close and sometimes had to tramp off into taller ferns and grasses under the trees, but Mercedes was good about staying to more open areas, as if she was used to having a person who couldn't trample through the underbrush as easily as she could.

I heard Ronette sigh a little.

"This is nothing," Lois said. "Searching can take hours."

I glanced at Ronette who just smiled at me. Scott said nothing but he looked ready to go back and sit down.

Mercedes pushed us onward. Fortunately the hills in the area were low and the brush wasn't too thick. This area had been semi-civilized for some time. We came to a break in the trees and looked over an overgrown field. Two old cars lay piled in a heap, all rust-brown and dented, the glass on the windshields and doors having long since broken out or been taken out. One had the hood up and there appeared to be more plants than machinery inside the engine compartment.

Beyond the cars, I saw an old square building in untreated wood, now kind of a brownish-gray. The building had stood out in the weather for a very long time with little or no upkeep.

Mercedes sniffed at the long grass and then detoured back into the wooded area, keeping to the edge until the overgrown field was behind us. I wasn't sure how far we were from the rest area parking lot. I could still hear cars on the freeway. A semi must have started up because I heard the hiss of brakes once.

We kept walking. The clouds shifted and the sun came out a little more. My southern blood soaked it up and wished it would stay longer. Mercedes headed into darker woods with more undergrowth. She dug around under a bush and came out with what looked like the bones of part of a hand.

"Scott?" Lois said quietly.

Scott came forward and squatted down, his hand against

a tree trunk to keep his balance. He looked more closely at what Mercedes had.

"Looks like part of a human hand," he said. "I'm not a forensic anthropologist, but I've seen hand bones in the office a time or two and that's definitely human and not an animal paw."

I took it to mean that at one time Scott had been a doctor.

Mercedes started whining and digging around near the plant. Lois called her over and gave her a treat. Mercedes ate it but then went back to look at the place and then looked at Lois and back to the bush. She couldn't have been more clear about wondering why Lois wasn't going over there to dig if she had a voice.

Lois got out a cell phone and started dialing. She seemed to know just who to call. Mercedes whined a little. Lois whispered that she should hush. I looked at the bone. It was surprisingly uneventful to find it. Did it belong to Lucy?

"No," the wind whispered at me.

I looked around. Ronette didn't seem to hear anything. She was looking a little creeped out by the hand bones which were on the ground near where Mercedes had found them.

Still, I had no doubt the words in the wind were meant for me.

LUCY: EARLY FALL THEN

The truck stank of cigarettes and Alma didn't let go of Lucy's arm, squeezing it so tightly, it would likely bruise. The bearded man didn't look at either of them as he navigated around the town. Lucy's heart sank when he took a narrow dirt road that ran off into a field.

When he stopped, Alma pulled Lucy out.

"You can walk back," Will said. He handed Alma a bunch of money. "If she's not useful to you after, I'll pay you more."

Alma smiled and nodded.

"This is what happens when you try and run away."

Lucy said nothing. No matter what happened, she wasn't going back to Alma. Maybe someone would find her and take her to a doctor or a hospital. They'd want to know why she was hurt so badly. She'd tell them. She'd tell them everything.

Will pushed her back against the tree and started stripping off her clothing.

"Why not your place?" she asked.

Will pulled out a knife. "I hate messes."

Lucy's eyes widened and her breath came faster, shallower. She shivered and not just because she was wet and cold.

Turning away she slipped away from the tree and started to run into the woods. If she could get far enough away to hide, she might have a chance.

She'd barely taken two steps when Will was on her. He wasn't just big. He was fast. Or maybe he'd just been expecting her to run so he was prepared. Lucy didn't know.

He pushed her down in the dirt and started tearing at her clothing, ripping the fabric with his teeth and hands, using the knife only when he had to.

Lucy screamed as loudly as she could.

She heard rustling in the underbrush, perhaps small creatures who wouldn't be able to help her leaving the area lest they be the next to be injured or worse.

The roughness, the way he grabbed her arms, too hard, too long, squeezing and twisting, guaranteeing a bruise, let Lucy know he didn't care if she were hurt. He paid for this.

Twisting her over so she faced him, Will placed a knee in her stomach, slowly lowering his weight so that Lucy couldn't get a breath in. And then he kneeled harder, forcing it down like he wanted her organs to pop out.

She groaned and whimpered which made him laugh.

Alma didn't care that this man tortured her so long as she was paid.

Lucy's sight went red. She was so angry that she was being used like this, tossed around, probably about to be killed, and her sister, the one person she had to count on, had put her in that position.

The anger let Lucy fight again. She started pounding and scratching and biting.

Now she wasn't the only one groaning and grunting.

Then, she was free to run. She didn't care that she had on only part of a shirt. Anger clouded her thoughts.

Distantly, Lucy heard cars traveling back and forth on the freeway. She ran towards that, not caring. She'd get away.

Branches grabbed at her, loyal soldiers to the bearded animal who roared behind her. Lucy kept running.

There was little for the branches to grab onto but her skin. She was so angry that she felt nothing. Blood began to pour down her right arm where a particularly viscous black-berry bush had gotten her.

Lucy ran. She was nearly to a clearing and then there was a thin line of trees and she'd be at the Pacific Highway.

She glanced back, startled to see Will so close behind, blood running down the side of his face, his teeth bared like a feral animal ready to attack.

Lucy ran harder but tripped in a hole, splaying down. Before she could get back up, Will was on her.

He used his fists first and then began to kick her. Lucy didn't see anything more, thankful he wasn't using the knife, certain he'd tire, expecting to wake after and make her way to the freeway. By the time the knife came out, she was too far gone to feel all the tiny cuts he made to in hopes of waking her to see her reaction to the pain. Eventually, tiring of his game, Will began to cut more deeply.

Lucy came briefly to consciousness one last time. She tried to fight the knife but everything hurt, her body already beginning to die, her brain offering her one last chance to try and save herself.

"I'll kill you. And I'll kill her too," she mumbled, too softly for Will to hear.

She would not wake up again.

31

TRACI: SEPTEMBER NOW

I don't know why I hadn't counted on the police and the time it would take them to arrive if we found something. I had this idea that if we found some bones, we'd dig them up and leave. Then I'd be free to do my ritual clearing and that would be that. Instead, we were asked to wait where we were, sending one of our party to the edge of the rest stop to lead officers to our location. Scott was the only one willing to leave to help out, though I worried about his ability to make the trek back, alone.

It began to drizzle, barely enough to wet the ground, but enough to add a chill to the air and make everything smell even more piney than it already did. Ronette wasn't bothered by the drips, nor was Lois. If anything, Mercedes seemed pleased by the rain and tried to start romping around, though Lois pulled her close in case the bones required forensic testing. If it was as old as I thought, it was likely that the only forensic evidence would be on the bones themselves.

I listened to Mercedes thrash and yip before settling down. The pine needles rustled and the branches swayed whenever the slightest breeze came up, leaving me shivering. I didn't remember the Northwest being that chilly, but I'd spent so long in North Carolina that I was beyond spoiled when it came to weather. Now I wore a jacket if it got below 72.

Ronette played on her phone.

"I had to text my husband that I wouldn't be home as quickly as I thought," she said. "He's supportive and all, but he'd hate it if I didn't let him know. I'll text the girls after they get home from school, when it's too late for them to get into anything huge without me there. They'll think if I don't let them know where I am, I'm on my way home and they won't make quite such a mess. If I wait, it'll be late enough that they'll worry about their dad coming home."

I laughed at the way her mind worked. It was quintessential Ronette, who was always thinking ahead and planning for what others might be thinking. It's what made her a great therapist. She'd been working only part-time while the girls were young and was looking forward to expanding her practice now that they were older. That was something we'd chatted about on Facebook because it was a safe topic and didn't require any judgements, unlike my issues with ghosts.

"I tried researching this area," Lois said. "I've been digging pretty deep and pulling in favors from the law officers who might remember things or maybe heard rumors from years ago. It's a tough one. I did have one officer recall that there was a guy named Will who lived in one of the little townships around here, off the beaten track, who had a reputation as one bad guy. He also said the Martin girl was into all kinds of stuff and was always barely making ends meet. She had quite a taste for alcohol, but he wasn't sure when that started. She'd been in jail and was out by the time he was in the force."

"So she wasn't very good at being a responsible adult?" I

asked. My impression from what I'd read was that neither Alma nor Lucy were very old.

"She didn't report her sister missing for a long time. In fact, she only did it because the school came around asking why she wasn't in school. At first Alma tried to say it was work but later on she said Lucy had run off. Didn't like working. No one had ever seen Lucy working, according to this officer, so it was assumed that her job was less than legal. In those days that would have meant prostitution."

It seemed like a very sad life to me, one that ended all too soon. I felt badly for Lucy, although I reminded myself that she wanted me dead for some twisted reason. Too bad the guy who murdered her was probably already dead. I had no idea what I was going to do to appease the girl.

"If she's out here, I wonder what happened," Ronette said. "This isn't close to anything."

"If she was turning tricks, they might have gone out in a car someplace where they wouldn't have been seen," Lois said.

"There's nothing for miles," Ronette said. "You'd think they could have gone a bit closer to town."

"Unless whoever killed her planned on killing her," I said softly. Again that feeling of sympathy.

It started to rain again, making Mercedes shake herself off a few feet away. She started to whine a bit. At first, I thought the rain was bothering her but soon enough, I heard the crack of branches and the faint sounds of people talking. A radio hissed and spat out some static. Scott was returning with the police.

We all turned, waiting, and were rewarded a short time later. Mercedes went running up to meet her other owner and let him know he'd been missed. It was hard not to smile at her enthusiastic, but polite, greeting.

"What have we got?" the officer was a tall man, thickly

built, but not fat, though in ten years he might be. His dark brown hair curled slightly over his ears. He was probably thinking about getting it cut to keep that from happening, particularly since he reached up and pushed it away multiple times as he spoke.

"We found this hand bone," Lois said, pointing at the bones sticking out from under the bush. Mercedes had dragged them that far before Lois had told her to drop, which she'd done quickly and without complaint. It was only then that Scott had squatted to identify that they looked human.

The office squatted down. A woman officer appeared at the edge of our makeshift clearing, watching. She'd clearly been scouting the perimeter of where we stood in case there were people waiting in ambush. Or at least that's what I thought. Maybe she needed to pee, and like me, hated rest areas.

"That looks like part of a human hand," the male officer said. He stood again, nodding at Scott, as if in apology for not believing him.

He walked to the side of the clearing and started talking into his radio. The woman came closer. She pushed the bushes aside, not stepping into the bones, the narrow fingers joined by a few traces of tissue that remained. She squatted down as low as she could and looked under the bush.

"Did you see how far the dog dragged the hand?"

The bushes weren't that thick, so I wasn't sure what she was getting at.

"She was just here. We've been trailing her through the woods, wherever she wants to go as much as we can," Lois said. "The hand wouldn't have been far under there."

"And what were you all doing out here again?" The officer asked, looking at each of us in turn.

Lois told her how she was one of those people who

looked at cold cases. I had an interest in finding a missing girl from the forties named Lucy Martin. I picked up the tale and explained that I was interested in her because of the women who had died at the rest area. I said I had once thought I was going to be attacked at Steely Woods years ago.

"Did you report it?" Officer Cross Your T's asked, probably wanting to check my story.

"I didn't," I said. "I lived in Portland at the time and it seemed pointless. Nothing happened."

Ronette said nothing.

"And you?" The woman looked at Ronette.

"I'm here for Traci. It didn't seem like a good idea to meet a stranger and a dog at a rest area without some support from a friend."

For the first time the woman officer smiled a little but then went back to picking apart our stories. Fortunately, Lois was being completely honest, and I had told this part of my story so many times it didn't matter. Ronette was being very good about volunteering nothing.

If the police didn't believe us, they said nothing. Of course, unless we were criminal masterminds using some sort of agent to break down flesh, the hand bones had been around for some time. Still, because this was a rest stop and we were traveling through, we were asked to wait.

Lois asked if she could take Mercedes for a bit of a walk back the way we had come. There was some discussion about whether this would be allowed, but in the end, Mercedes got to burn off some of her energy. Scott found a log to sit on a bit away from the little clearing, though his jacket was still visible from where we were.

Ronette and I huddled near a tree and tried to stay dry when the rain got heavier.

Eventually a detective arrived with another officer and asked us more of the same questions we'd been asked before.

Another group of people arrived checking out the bone and looking around the area for other clues. At that point, our personal information was taken and we were escorted back to the rest area.

"Well, that was exciting," Lois said. She was still smiling.

I looked at Ronette who just sort of nodded.

"I need to use the restroom," Ronette said before we got to the car. I watched her go inside.

It was later in the afternoon and a few women went in and came back out, but no Ronette. The back of my neck started to tingle. My stomach started to knot. I worried she was in trouble.

I hung back but walked closer, the door like a maw that opened into hell.

The two men serving coffee had been replaced by a man and a woman, both equally old. They seemed interested in the police cars that were parked off to one side, where we'd all entered the woods.

I took a deep breath. The air felt too cold and tasted of old bitter coffee. I didn't care. I needed to go check on Ronette.

I waited until a red-haired woman in a blue skirted suit got out of a car and walked quickly to the building. I headed in behind her.

Ronette was at the dryer, which wasn't blowing on her hands and she was shaking them out.

"Sorry," she said. "I knew it was taking a while but I didn't realize it was so long that you had to come in."

"What happened?" I asked as we left the place. I hated the smell of it and even by day it reminded of the last time I'd been in there, not something I wanted to think about. I hurried out.

"The dryer wasn't working. Everyone seems fine with wet

hands but I hate that," Ronette said. She was rubbing her slightly damp hands together. "There was air but no heat."

I saw her look over at the people offering coffee.

"Think we should tell them?" I asked.

Ronette shrugged. "I'm sure they'll find out soon enough. We should get going."

She had a long drive head of her. I'd probably have dinner at Burger King and then some wandering around before I came back after dark to do my ritual.

My stomach plunged to my feet. I was going to be alone for the ritual and I had no idea if it would work. I started worrying about being interrupted by the police, perhaps even being accused of being responsible for the bones we'd found earlier.

The worries ate away at me, keeping me from hearing anything Ronette said during the rest of our drive back to the Burger King. If she noticed, she didn't make any comments

32

TRACI: SPRING, WHEN IT HAPPENED

It all happened the night after Ronette's birthday. I'd come up to Tacoma, where she'd lived. It had been for a girl's night party where we'd driven to a trendy area and we had drinks at bunch of bars, laughing and singing and having a good time. I knew I was driving back when we were done so I'd been the designated driver, slogging back too many Diet Cokes, laughing as hard as anyone.

The friendly low cream buildings that greeted me during the day had changed to something more ominous when I got to Steely Woods, a pit stop I had been aching for for miles. I'd considered stopping along the freeway and going in the bushes, but I wasn't quite that brave. Besides, I knew the trip. I knew the rest stop wasn't that far ahead.

Pulling off into the parking area, the previously friendly buildings looked haunted. Instead of being welcoming, the trees at Steely Woods stood pale and skeletal in the late winter night. A light breeze made the branches drift like dancing ghosts. The evergreens were mere shadows behind the dancers, swaying in time.

Across the grassy area that housed the toilets and the

little office, I saw three semis parked. There was one other car on my side of the lot, parked as far from the buildings as possible. It sat dark and lonely. The rest stop allowed no camping but that didn't mean you couldn't take a quick nap in your car.

I jumped at the sound of a bang against the driver's side window, not sure what made it. I saw nothing. The skeletal trees continued their dance. Perhaps a gust of wind. I took a breath in to calm my heart. There was something about the rest stop at night, and me there alone, which made the hairs on the back of my neck stand up.

With my bladder nearly bursting, I doubted I'd make it to the next off ramp before my need moved beyond critical. I got out. The wind flowed softly around me, not the sort of wind that gusts and bangs against glass. The smell of pine reached my nose laced with that of old French fries. I walked past the dumpsters, noticing that they were full. Three French fries lay on the ground.

I continued to the building. The window in the office, where coffee was normally served, gaped like a dark mouth. Out on the freeway beyond the stop, the sound of a semi braking could have been a sigh.

I hurried into the bathroom. I just wanted this to be done. The bathroom was well lit and clean. The stall doors were all closed, but I saw no feet in any of them. I picked one at random, one not too far from the door, and went in to do my business.

A faucet dripped, just once. It echoed too loudly in the silent room.

Down the way, in another stall, I heard a light tap as if someone moved. I looked under the wall but saw no feet. Maybe a mouse or something. I *was* out in nowhere. I sat.

Someone banged open a stall door at the far end of the bathroom. The crash of the door echoed in the quiet. I jumped. Another crash echoed as the next door banged, coming closer. I looked under the edge of my stall but could see no feet. The next stall door banged open.

That stopped all possibility of doing my business. I waited. I wanted nothing more than to pull up my jeans and run, but I was frozen where I sat. Fear ramped up my need even as it paralyzed me, keeping me from doing anything. The door to the stall next to mine banged open. My door would be next.

I saw a hand at the top of my door. I heard something that could have been a groan, but lower and softer.

The hand moved, getting a better grip. The long fingers, skeletal in their thinness, looked the color of the bone in the harsh light. The nails were short and pointed. If the bathroom hadn't been so well-lit, I would have said the hand was a claw. Then another hand appeared, pale and thin. It matched its companion, but for one blackened nail on the pinky finger as if it had been slammed in one of the doors it banged against.

I stopped breathing, waiting for what would happen next. Slowly I saw the hairs on a head, unevenly spaced and sparse, appear as if someone were raising themselves up to look over the door. As the head began to appear, I saw that the hair wasn't just sparse, it was patchy, like someone had pulled large handfuls of it out.

At that point my bladder let go. Fortunately, I was on the toilet because I had no ability to stop anything. My legs had no more control than my bladder. Had I been standing, attempting to run, I knew I couldn't have supported my weight. My heart tried to beat its way out of my chest. The skull that was beneath those tufts of hair was as pale as the claws that grasped the door. Whatever was beyond the door was not human.

I was going to die sitting on a toilet at the Steely Woods Rest Stop a month before my twenty-sixth birthday.

Even as my lungs burned and my bladder emptied its contents, the skull crept ever closer to looking over the top of the stall door. Just as it was about to peer over, letting me look into eyes that were no doubt deep black pits, the main bathroom door squeaked open.

"I cannot believe it!" a girl said, giggling.

"I know!" another girl said.

"Hurry up. Mom doesn't like stopping here at night," the first one said.

They trooped loudly through the silence of the bathroom. My heart was the only other sound thundering along with them. The creature was gone. This was my escape. I saw the girl's feet when they tramped by. One girl had on green sneakers with rainbow socks. The other girl was in plain blue and white trainers with socks that weren't visible between shoe and jeans. Ordinary.

They loudly banged stall doors, closing and latching them shut. This time the sound was comforting rather than frightening.

They had saved me. At least for the moment. I finished by business in record time. I didn't bother to wash my hands, merely hurried out to my car.

There were three dark drops on the asphalt by where I'd parked. I hadn't noticed them getting out of the car, didn't really notice them going back in except to wonder if they could have been blood. Whose blood I didn't know.

My hands shook so hard I couldn't find my keys. It took four tries to get the door unlocked because I kept missing the hole.

There was one other car in the lot now, a silver gray Accord with a woman sitting in it, the engine running, a calming purr in the background. The trees no longer danced. The breeze didn't tug at my hair.

I climbed in the car, afraid the engine wouldn't start, breathing a sigh of relief when it did. While I had had a hard time finding where to put the keys, the engine started on the first try.

I drove out, watching as the girls hurried out of the bathroom, heading happily towards their car, never noticing the shadowed figure that huddled behind them. I thought I saw a flash of white teeth, too large and too even to be real, but I looked away, certain I was imagining things.

I practically flew home to Portland that night, always certain that there was someone behind me, chasing me. Once I thought I saw a face in the rearview mirror, partly rotten and boney, but it was gone as soon as I noticed it.

I whimpered. I kept the radio on as loudly as it would go just to keep me company while hoping the noise would fool whatever it was that was after me into thinking I wasn't actually alone on the nearly empty freeway late at night.

Perhaps it had been fooled because it never attacked me, though I had no doubt, years later, that it had followed me and bided its time, angry perhaps at being interrupted.

33

TRACI: SEPTEMBER NOW

I drove across the street from the Burger King to a McDonald's. It's not that I don't like Burger King, but I'd had that for lunch with Ronette. Now that I was back at the exit, I didn't have much to do with myself. Ronette was heading home, dreading having to have the discussion with her husband about what exactly she'd been doing out at the rest stop with me.

I stayed at the exit with the fast food places, a couple of gas stations, and an old hotel that had once been nice, but now appeared to be the kind of place I wasn't at all keen on staying at. Heavier traffic rumbled down the freeway. Friday night and people were heading for far places or perhaps just heading home after a day at work. Living in downtown Charlotte, I had forgotten how many people commuted. Even in Charlotte, commutes tended to be shorter in distance if not in time.

The air around me smelled surprisingly clean and dry, like the rain that had plagued us in the woods had moved on. Still, plenty of gray clouds darkened the skies as the day headed towards evening. It made me wonder about the timing of the ritual. I wondered if I should wait until midnight or if I could start earlier, perhaps shortly after the rest stop quieted down for the evening.

Thinking about going back there made my stomach churn. McDonald's no longer sounded good. No food sounded good, and if I kept thinking about what I needed to do, I'd be forced to choose between vomiting in their toilets or out in the parking lot. I'm sure the manager wouldn't appreciate either, particularly since I hadn't been a customer.

I breathed in and out and started the car. I wasn't going to eat anything. I didn't even want a soda, not really. I made my way to the freeway to head south, back to the rest stop.

I had Ronette on speed dial, though I knew she'd be too far away to help me if something went wrong—if I was even able to call her. Unless someone showed up at just the right time, I would be on my own.

That thought sent shivers down my spine. I was on the on-ramp, speeding up even as the car climbed the incline to I-5. It was too late to turn back.

I knew all of this. I didn't need to keep reminding myself that this was mine to do and mine alone. I'd avoided this confrontation for years. I could have stayed that night, after the girls and their mother left and confronted the ghost then. Maybe just seeing her for what she was would have been enough.

Or perhaps I could have gone home and studied up on what had happened and then come back a few weeks later and confronted the ghost. Another woman, maybe two, would still be alive today. I'd likely never have met Deborah because if I hadn't been on the run, I would never have moved to North Carolina.

I tried to think of what else I might have missed, but sadly, I'd been so shut in, so completely terrified of every-thing, I hadn't made a life. I'd missed my life, missed having children, having a long term relationship, having a closer relationship with the sister I loved. If I had confronted the ghost sooner, maybe I'd have lived closer, in Las Vegas or down in Phoenix, though I couldn't really see myself in the desert. Perhaps I'd have gone to Colorado to live in the mountains. Hard to say.

Maybe I'd have gotten on a plane to go see her and the plane would have crashed. So many what ifs. I couldn't turn back the clock. I could only go forward.

Although there were plenty of cars, they moved along easily, tires eating away at the asphalt that led ever further south to Portland, to Eugene, to Sacramento and beyond. I wondered what it would feel like to keep driving.

Ronette would be unhappy with me. Or perhaps not. She seemed to understand how terrified I was. She also seemed to understand that this was something I had to do myself.

I tapped the steering wheel when I saw the first blue sign indicating a rest area was coming up. I hadn't left the right hand lane, not needing to go any faster, not really wanting to get to the place any sooner than I had to.

The exit came far too soon. I remembered the night when I'd had to pee, thinking that it took forever between the blue sign that said rest area 1 mile and actually getting there. Tonight, it took no time at all. I'd hardly registered that the sign was there.

Evergreens still lined the entrance, unchanged from earlier, though they looked more ominous. A few stately deciduous trees of a sort I couldn't identify stood sentinel with their long boney branches reaching out to the cars.

A half dozen vehicles sat in the parking area. There were more semis in the truck park across the way. A police cruiser waited in the corner of the parking area, perhaps someone guarding what had once been a crime scene or a lone officer finishing up his paperwork in the car.

I parked a little ways away from the building, towards the cruiser. I watched as people talked and smoked outside the building. A few hurried back to cars. Two other cars followed me in and their owners got out to use the restroom.

A woman opened her car door and leashed her dog, a long low dog, perhaps a dachshund, though it was wider than the dachshunds I knew. She led it across the wide parking lot and into the dog area.

I sat in my car watching.

The radio blared static, startling me and I jumped.

"Don't get too comfortable tonight!" a voice said and then cut out to static which faded into the background.

I glared at the station. I wasn't at all comfortable. But Lucy, if that's who it was, didn't need to remind me. I was like a mouse to her cat, thinking I was setting a trap but she was determined to make sure I knew that she knew about my plans. Or maybe she didn't and was hoping I'd give them away.

I turned the radio off and it stayed silent. That left me alone with the sounds of the people driving in and out of the rest stop. Another police car pulled up, perhaps to spell the officer in the corner. I watched in the rearview mirror. No one noticed me.

It got darker. Eventually, traffic thinned. I started to feel as if I needed to use the restroom, but I didn't dare. I'd go in the bushes before I'd go inside, unless I had an armed guard that I trusted, and, at this point, I didn't trust anyone.

The number of cars stopping in slowed as the evening wore on. Those that were there stayed a bit longer, people standing and stretching. I waited, not getting out of the car. I played with my phone some, but not too much. I needed a decent charge for when I was alone. I ran the car off and on to charge it back up.

Pretty soon the only other people around were the police

cars, of which there were still two cars, and the semis across the way. One of the police cars drove off. I was almost alone on my side of the rest stop.

I got out and went to the trunk to gather the things I'd need for the ritual together. No one was around to notice me. I wondered briefly if the police car had been abandoned. Even if it wasn't, which was most likely, the officer clearly wasn't around this part of the rest stop. I continued on searching for what I needed.

I checked my phone for the list I'd compiled from Will's suggestions. For a moment, I longed to call him, to talk it through, to gather courage, but I was equally certain that talking to anyone would allow me to put off going in to the rest room and doing the ritual.

I sighed, stretching. I glanced around.

The truckers were all clearly visible in their cabs, the lights shining just right. No one walked around the grounds. I was as alone as I was going to get. I shivered.

A breeze came up, light but still there, making the pine needles rattle and the branches sing. The automatic lights around the buildings looked yellow in the night. It wasn't so different from the time I'd been attacked.

It was now or never.

34

TRACI: SEPTEMBER NOW

I now had one bag with everything I thought I needed. I also had an electric lantern and my phone. I locked my purse, except for the car keys, into the trunk. I pulled out some of the metal spoons and lined my bra with them, feeling foolish standing by the car, messing with my breasts. If the truckers watched, they probably had an interesting show. Finished, I walked slowly towards the restrooms, the one on the left side, the one where I had nearly died on a night not unlike this one.

That night I'd smelled French fries. Tonight I smelled stale coffee and damp. I reminded myself that a police officer wasn't far away. If I had to scream, I had a good chance someone would hear me and come running and help, even if the truckers didn't.

I also knew that the officer was probably too far away to be of help. Really, I was on my own.

I wore sneakers which squeaked against the lightly damp pavement. It wasn't raining any longer but the concrete hadn't had time to dry. A few puddles by the gutter remained, a reminder of the earlier showers. The sound of my shoes echoed in the night as if the very air believed I didn't belong there.

I continued towards the building, listening. The hair on the back of my neck stood up but no one followed me. If a presence lurked behind me, it made no move to touch me, not then.

In the circle of buildings I was more protected from the light breeze, but the air there felt still and expectant, as if I'd walked in on something I had no business knowing about.

I chanted "Go away," under my breath. As if that would help. I had no belief in the chant. I wore my sterling silver bracelet and my bra lined with spoons. Not that I could do much with a spoon, but if steel worked, my heart would be protected.

I walked through the doorway of the restroom. The white tile glared back at me in lights that buzzed too loudly. The dryers waited for someone to wash their hands. I looked down, peering below the stalls, ascertaining the room was empty. I smelled the faint scent of dirty diaper and something else, something older and rotten.

I pulled out my salt and sprinkled a circle around me.
The faucet dripped.
Once.
I didn't see which one.
Paper rustled from far down the stalls, like someone pulling out a seat protector. The room went silent.

I said a prayer, a real prayer of the sort I hadn't said in years. Not since I'd tried to bury myself in the church in hopes of cutting ties to this terror. Now I was facing it… and I was alone. I wasn't as terrified as I expected, but perhaps I'd lived with this level of terror for so long I no longer noticed. I did not, however, speak any words aloud.

I lit several candles and placed them around the circle.
I called upon the angels and God.

Something moved in the far stall.

I heard, but didn't see the stall door open and bang shut. By the time I turned I saw only the door slowly swinging shut.

"Be gone," I whispered again. I still had no faith in what I was doing.

I held the sharpest of the stainless steel knives I had, waiting. I used a bit of my regular old bottled water to cover it and then poured salt all over the thing. It might not be holy water but if salt could stop the creature at the circle, then perhaps if it got closer I could cut it with a knife covered in salt.

I waited. The stillness, the waiting, made my stomach hurt and groan. Every muscle tensed against something I couldn't see. I wasn't sure how long I could continue, my muscles already beginning to strain. I wanted to relax, to give over to the ache but I couldn't. I had to wait.

Part of me wanted to rush down through the stalls, bang them open, find the creature, and stab it with the knife. The other side wanted the story. Why me? Why the woman who had died. Why Deborah? Why? Just why.

"Why do you do this Lucy?" I called. I thought I spoke in a room voice, my regular talking voice, but instead it came out a hoarse whisper, as if I didn't have enough air to speak.

"Because I can," the wind whispered to me, a chattering of branches like bone on bone and a slight breeze. It even lifted my hair.

"Not an answer," I growled. I really did sound like I was growling. If someone came in, they'd probably report me and not just for making a mess with salt and candles in the rest area.

"Do you know what I went through?" A howling screech of wind and the sound of words hit me. I was bent forward, nearly having to step out of the circle, which I realized too late, that I had made too small.

"Tell me."

"Betrayal. Betrayer. I will kill her."

"Who? Alma?" I asked.

"Who else? Sister who was not sister. Who gave me over to die." The wind was no longer there. The voice was hollow and solid. The hairs on my arms stood up. I should have been more terrified but the fact that she wanted to talk calmed me slightly.

"Alma is dead, Lucy," I said. "It's been years. She died years ago."

There was no response to that.

I lit the sage, letting it burn in the cup. I was supposed to sage the whole place but I wasn't stepping out of the questionable protection of the circle.

No voices. I might have been there alone.

Eventually, as the sage burned and filled the area I was in with the spicy aroma of smoke, I did step out. I carried the sage and the iron knife.

I walked to the back of the room and started with the large disabled stall, swinging the sage around the space.

Nothing appeared to me in there. No sounds of a ghost screaming in agony as it lost its grip on this world.

I saged the stall next to the larger stall at the end.

Nothing.

I breathed a little easier. Maybe I was doing something.

Maybe Lucy was done.

I saged the next stall and the next. I came to the one I had used. I breathed a little harder but when I opened it, it was empty.

I used the sage.

One of the faucets dripped.

One.

My breath hitched.

I heard something in the far stall. A sound like someone waited in there.

I backed up as quickly as I could, towards my salt circle, hoping to make it, to re-place the salt where I had scattered it when I'd stepped over it.

A thing, a gross and distorted bundle of bones and rags flew towards me. I had a moment to make out a few stray hairs on top of a skull a dull brown and beige as well as long white fingers made of bone reaching for me.

I couldn't move fast enough. I held the sage in one hand and the iron knife in the other.

I smelled burning flesh, felt a cold chill surround me and as suddenly as it came, it was gone.

I backed up further towards the salt circle.

"Be gone," I said.

I glanced behind me but there was nothing. My heart hammered from fear but also from exhilaration. I had faced Lucy and won.

35

TRACI: SEPTEMBER NOW

I wanted to laugh and to giggle. I wasn't done. There was still one more stall to sage. And Lucy was clearly still around despite the sage clearing of the final stall. There was something else I had to do.

"Did we find your bones this afternoon Lucy?" I asked. I spoke out loud. Though I hadn't yelled, it seemed too loud for the silence of the restroom. Had I really been alone in there all that time?

I waited, listening. There was only me, the faintest purr of cars along I-5, and the smell of sage, which was far better than the faint scent of dirty diaper.

I saw nothing. It was cool in the restroom but not cold, not like I had been in that instant that Lucy should have reached me and perhaps torn out my throat or maybe my femoral artery.

"Lucy?" I asked again when she still didn't answer.

"I am more than bones," the voice said. This time it wasn't the wind whispering. This time there was a chill against my right ear and a sound that came from behind. I whirled, holding the sage and the knife but there was nothing.

"But don't you want to have it known what happened to you?" I asked.

"No one knows. No one blamed Alma or the one who murdered me," Lucy said. "And it's too late. I'll never have peace. She might have gotten away, but I will make sure you don't."

"But they're clearly dead too," I said. "Can't you deal with them on your side?"

There was something like laughter, a canned sort of clacking of something like bone against bone that reached me.

"I don't know what happens after death," I said. "But we can't help you here."

"And so people will continue to die. People here and the people around you."

"That doesn't seem fair," I said. Weren't there laws?

"Was it fair what happened to me?" This was anger. I felt it brush through me, trying to gain traction in my soul. Anger at all the things that had happened to me, at all the things I had missed. At Ronette for not being there when I needed her, even if I was the one who had pushed her away. She should have known.

I heard a car door slam.

And then there was nothing.

The soft squelch of sneakers against damp concrete and then against tile.

Ronette appeared in the doorway.

"Traci?" she said quietly.

I must have looked insane. I felt insane. A circle of salt at my feet, holding a bundle of sage and an iron knife ready to stab anyone who got too close to me.

"Ronette?" I asked. "What are you doing here?"

And before I could do anything, without even the warning of a faucet dripping, the thing that was Lucy rushed out of the back stall, coming towards Ronette instead of me.

I stepped in front of the flying creature, using the knife, jamming upwards, waving the sage randomly with my left hand.

It wasn't an intentional wave. I was just moving around, trying to keep my balance. This time, I felt like I had hit something.

Whatever it was, it continued to press towards me, pushing me back.

I held my ground as much as I could, though I felt myself falling backwards.

"Run!" I screamed.

I heard something moving, wasn't sure it if was Ronette or Lucy or what was left of Lucy.

Then I was on my back, the cold hard tile pressing into my spine. I hurt. I still held the knife but now it held bits of flesh and something white flecked the edge. I pushed myself up.

The sage burned low. I was going to run out soon. I wondered if it had done anything at all.

I looked around, but didn't see Ronette, didn't see what I feared, a body lying down, dead with cuts all over her, cuts that the police might think were made by my knife, when in actuality they were made by nothing anyone could see.

I heard weeping outside.

I hurried out.

Ronette was pressed against the brick of the building, sniffling and crying. She wasn't crying loudly, only sniffling.

"How could you stand there and work with that?" she asked.

"I was trying to get rid of it," I said.

"I know. But how?" Ronette wasn't making sense. She paused, looking at me. "How could you ever face it again?

I've never been so scared. I thought I got your terror but this…"

She was shaking her head.

On some level she'd never quite believed me. Thought, perhaps, that I'd had some sort of incident and like Anson was saying, I had made up something to fit the facts. Now she had seen it and knew it was real, knew I wasn't making anything up at all and it terrified her.

"I had to do it," I said. "She said she'd keep hurting people close to me and I'm hoping to take care of her."

Ronette nodded. "I came back to make sure you were okay. But I can't go back in there. I'm sorry."

"I'll call you when I'm done," I said.

Ronette nodded but she made no move to go to her car. She continued shaking. I wanted to help her, but I would have to put down one of my items, either the knife or the sage. I wasn't willing to do either of those things. I was certain they were the reason I was standing up.

One of my spoons shifted in my bra and dug into my chest. Reassuring in some bizarre way. I went back into the building to continue to do battle.

"Why only women?" I asked out loud when I was standing near the salt I had poured. One of the candles had gutted. I'd knocked another over and fortunately, instead of lighting the place on fire, it had gutted against the tile. Maybe the building did need to burn.

I kept that in mind. I didn't have what it would take to burn the place down, not then but if I had to, I would.

"Why women Lucy? Why them?"

"She *betrayed* me," the voice said. So much anger.

"But it was a man who murdered you," I replied. I looked around, trying to see where she might be, what I might need to do to burn the place down. Of course the building was brick, filled with tile and metal. Burning would be difficult, if not impossible. Maybe if one of those semi's exploded over it but probably not without something that drastic.

"She was my *sister*." The anger was giving way to pain.

"She should have protected you." I tried to remember what I had picked up reading pop-psychology books during my enforced imprisonment of fear.

There was nothing.

"Let me take you. You'll be the last. I promise."

The voice was close, near my ear again. The chill was sinking down into my shoulder, making my right arm, the one with the knife feel heavy. I felt lethargic, as if I wanted to lie down and give in.

"No more," I said. "Begone!" I whirled whipping the knife around. Again, I felt I encountered something almost solid, the knife slipping through. This time the force was the same as hitting softened butter. There, but not there. A tugging that could have been my imagination but I'd given up believing Lucy was only my imagination hours ago, if not years.

And then Lucy stood before me, on the other side of the salt. She was a girl, younger than I was, perhaps not much younger than I had been the first time I'd nearly died in the rest area. She was underdressed in thin jeans and a shirt with long sleeves, the cuffs frayed. A rip showed me part of her belly, thin and sunken. A button had been sewn on with a brighter colored thread. Her feet were in old faded red, now pink, Keds that looked worn and in need of repair, the sole splitting from the pink fabric on one side.

"She locked me in to keep me from going to school or getting help. Then she chased me down and gave me to him," Lucy said. She was a child, angry, spitting mad, wanting to be heard.

"I can try and write up your story so people know," I said. "Is that what you want? Would that do?"

"I was a person!" Lucy screamed.

"I know." She looked sad.

Suddenly I was overwhelmed by sadness, a wave of it, engulfing me. I had heard the term, thought it cliché, but in that moment a wave was exactly what it was. An emotion so large and so big it might have been the ocean crashing down over me, threatening to drown me in pain. I gasped, unable to catch my breath. I fought the pain, struggling to come up for air.

"He beat me nearly to death," Lucy said. "And then he used me. After, he used the knife. And she let him. For money."

"That was wrong," I said, feeling rather sick and not just from the sorrow I was feeling. No wonder this girl was so angry.

Lucy reached out a hand. I was tempted to take it, to drop the sage and take it but I didn't move.

"I'm sorry," I said. "I can't trust you. Not after all you've done. All you've threatened. I will tell your story though. You deserve that."

The face changed, morphing into the half decomposed corpse it had been. I wondered why she chose that and not the bones she was likely reduced to by now.

She flew at me, the breeze sending the salt flying around the room. I snapped my eyes shut to avoid getting any in them. I held up the sage and the knife. Nothing hit me.

I tried to breathe but the salt was still in the air making it taste of the sea and sage and I couldn't draw air. I backed up, into a cold embrace.

It tightened on me and something sliced through my skin, hitting the iron of the spoon. It withdrew as suddenly as it was there.

I whirled with the knife out, slicing through the apparition. I didn't aim but caught the bones near the shoulder and the neck.

Lucy's eyes widened.

I withdrew the knife.

Her skeletal mouth seemed to widen its smile, though I knew that had to be my imagination and the shadows in the room, such as they were.

I drew the knife across where her neck would be, plunging it deep enough to reach the boney neck.

Her head tottered and slid to the side.

I thought I heard a scream of pain.

I backed up.

The lights buzzed more loudly. I saw a bright orange spark just as the room went black.

I froze, listening.

I heard nothing at first. I waited, my eyes adjusting to the blackness. The faintest light come from the doorway.

I made my way there, worried I'd step on a pile of bones and they'd reach up and grab me. Through the door, the parking lot was equally dark. The parked cars were dark.

I didn't see Ronette.

I looked at the cars, hoping to see someone in one of them, perhaps playing a radio or using a phone and offering a bit of light, but the only light that came was the periodic swath of headlines from the freeway as people passed by.

I saw something move near Ronette's car. I hurried over there.

Ronette was leaning down. I heard her retch.

"What is it?" I asked.

She shook her head. "I saw a head go flying, like it had been lopped off. There's blood…" She pointed at the ground but seemed confused when she couldn't find any drops of blood around. Whatever she had seen was gone.

"I think she's gone," I said.

"No," Ronette said. "I think she fled."

I said nothing, knowing she'd continue. Ronette nodded to the trees. There was no breeze. In fact, it was too still. The air felt almost humid, pregnant as it was with waiting.

Lucy was out there. Where I'd need to finish it. I turned on my phone for a light, handing the sage to Ronette. I was pretty sure the iron knife had done the work but I couldn't to leave my friend unprotected, or at least not completely unprotected.

"I have stuff in the restroom I might need."

Ronette nodded, preparing to wait.

I walked back to the restroom. I didn't dread the walk the way I had earlier. In fact, it was almost easy. Almost, but not quite. My body still tensed, my insides shaking. I hated the way the hairs on my neck stayed raised, telling me that someone was behind me, though I was fairly certain that no one was. I hated the stillness and the quietness of the night.

But I had faced down my ghost and I had lived. She was still after me, but I knew I could survive another encounter.

I used my phone to find my things, locating the lantern I'd taken with me. I turned that on to save my phone's battery. The candles had all burned down so I packed them up, along with my salt. I left the restroom to go out to the woods and finalize the ceremony.

"What about the cop?" I asked Ronette.

"What cop?" Ronette asked.

I nodded at the squad car that sat in the shadows.

I carried the lantern and the iron knife. Ronette followed with the sage.

"You don't have to come," I said. I wasn't sure how I'd carry everything but I'd make do if I had to.

"I need to see this through," Ronette said. "The head sailed by but as it did so, something touched me, like a hand but it was so cold, I was sure I had frost bite on my arm. It makes me shudder just to think about it, like a really gross bug was crawling on your skin."

I pictured a tarantula crawling up my arm and tried to keep myself from shivering. Ronette knew how I hated spiders and I was glad she hadn't given voice to that particular fear when she described her experience.

We set off towards the path we had taken earlier. I hoped that we could find our way to the place Mercedes had found the bones.

Walking was harder in the dark, even with the lantern. A few creatures scurried out of the way, but for the most part the night was silent except for Ronette and me traipsing through the underbrush. Everything seemed a little too loud, like we were trying to sneak up on someone and failing miserably.

Suddenly it brightened to my right. Probably the lights from the rest area going back on. If there was an electrical problem, it was fixed. If it was Lucy, perhaps she decided there was no reason to leave the place in the dark.

It seemed to take longer to get to the place where we'd stopped earlier, but perhaps I'd taken us in a few circles. Finally, though, I saw yellow police tape. The bushes had been pulled up and overturned. A hole had been dug. No bones remained, but I figured any that had been found had been taken to the morgue or wherever you take old bones found near a rest stop.

I drew a breath. I heard Ronette do the same.

It was cold there. Colder than it should have been. I turned.

Ronette wasn't behind me. Lucy was.

36

TRACI: SEPTEMBER NOW

I screamed. Short and loud and then cut off because my chest tightened and I had no air to scream again.

Lucy was in her half decomposed look, her head tilted at a wild angle giving her the look of someone who had been nearly decapitated. Maybe that was exactly what happened. I didn't know. However, it reminded me of what I'd done to her spirit when I'd lashed at her with my knife.

My hands shook and I dropped the bag that I carried in the hand with the lantern. I searched around, hoping to see Ronette. I worried that she'd never really been there at all or worse, that Lucy had gotten to her as we walked through the woods.

"Be gone," I said. My voice shook. I no longer had any confidence. It wasn't just me. It was Ronette I needed to save. Even if our conversation had been an illusion Lucy set up, that meant Ronette was in danger.

"Make me," Lucy said. Her skull grinned at me.

Her hand reached out, a long boney finger, one scrap of brown skin still stuck to the edge and a nail that was partially broken on the pinkie finger. She tried to scratch me but I stepped back. I felt the flutter of the police tape behind my legs. The hole wasn't far beyond and I hoped I didn't end up falling into it.

I nearly vomited. I'd be falling into Lucy's grave.

I held up the knife and swung it towards the arm but Lucy had already pulled back.

She rushed at me, faster than I would have expected, going low, like she was after my gut.

I swung the knife low. Felt it collide with something. I fell backwards, landing on my butt just beyond the police tape.

I got to my knees, noting my bag wasn't far. I didn't see Lucy anywhere.

I grabbed my bag hoping to find matches. I worked one handed in case Lucy came back for me.

I had to try and pry open the bag and get my arm inside with one hand. The plastic wanted to stick together. Finally I had my arm in there. The candle was an easy find by the shape. I grabbed that and set it out on the ground.

I grabbed the salt next. I poured that around, a small circle for me to sit inside, just in case it helped.

Then I found the matches. To light them, I'd have to put down the knife for a minute. I looked around, waiting.

The air was still but something moved in the brush near me. Tiny scurryings like small creatures, maybe a mouse. An owl hooted somewhere. I felt the slightest breeze against my neck. I breathed. Everything in the woods seemed normal.

I put down the knife.

I pulled out a match and struck it on the box. Nothing. I hit it again.

This time it lit.

I held it to the candle but a breeze came up and gutted it before it was lit.

I tossed the old match and tried again. This time it lit on the first try, the flame burning bright in the darkness. I touched it to the candle. Once again a breeze came up just in time to gut the flame.

Lucy didn't want me to light the darned thing.

That made me more determined than ever.

I worked at it again and again, going through five matches before I was able to angle my hand so that the candle didn't gut as soon as I lit it.

Something ran at me, low, where I was kneeling.

I held the candle and I pressed it towards the thing coming at me. I felt a rush of wind, but while the flame flickered, it didn't go out.

I turned to see if what might be behind me.

Nothing.

I stood up, still holding the candle instead of the knife and looked around. Nothing.

I set the candle down near the grave and picked up the knife.

"I'm sorry for all that was done to you," I said. "I'm sorry you didn't get a chance to live the life you wanted and deserved to live. I'm sorry you weren't found, that it sounds like no one mourned you. I'll mourn you and make sure you are remembered. Let your spirit be gone!"

I didn't know where the words came from. They were what I was feeling. I was both terrified of what Lucy was doing and sad for her. I was angry that I was in the line of fire, worried for Ronette, but still sympathetic to what had happened to the poor girl.

"What the hell are you doing out here?" I turned to see a young man in a police uniform.

"Just saying a prayer for the bones you found," I said, hoping he hadn't heard what I'd said and question me.

"You're beyond the police tape." He didn't seem happy about that.

Just then the wind picked up. Really picked up and started

shaking the leaves and the breeze. As suddenly as it started, it stopped.

Silence. Even the creatures who had been scurrying away had gone silent.

The officer noticed it. He licked his lips once. In the pale light of the lantern and his flashlight he looked a sickly yellow pale. His hair was plastered to his head as if he'd been out in the rain, or maybe he purposefully slicked it down, I wasn't sure. He looked from side to side, his hand going to his gun, though he didn't draw it.

I looked around too, waiting.

There it was. A hollow scream of the sort I've never heard before. I didn't know how any voice could make such a sound.

Lucy appeared at the edge of the trees. Her skull remained only partly tacked on her head. She rushed the officer.

If he could have gotten any paler he would have. He backed up towards me, away from her. I leaped in front of him, wielding the knife. Lucy stopped.

"Broken circle. Bad little wanna-be witch," she said. "Don't think there haven't been others trying to purify this space. It can't be purified. I don't want to be purified"

"What the hell?" the deputy mumbled behind me.

I didn't turn. Lucy rushed both of us. I felt her push me into the deputy and he stepped back, into the hole. I fell with him, landing on top of him. Fortunately the knife was out front of me. Lucy stood at the edge of the hole, looking down at us. We weren't that deep, perhaps a foot and a half.

I scrambled off the deputy, holding the knife out towards Lucy.

"Oh fuck… Oh fuck…" he was lying there. He rolled over. I glanced at him. Saw the white bone sticking up through the dirt. Saw the tear in side of his shirt, a small hole where the bone poked through.

There wasn't a ton of blood and he didn't look as if he'd punctured anything.

He was trying to get someone on the radio but all I head was static. Lucy stood there waiting.

The deputy gave up and fired at her three times.

Lucy rushed at us.

I cut with the knife.

The deputy kept firing at her, one bullet going so close to me I felt the heat of its passing along my arm. Just what I needed. A scared deputy who thought he could shoot a ghost.

I held my ground with my knife, which I was certain was more deadly to her than the gun. Or perhaps not. But I knew I could hurt her form with it, though I didn't know if I actually hurt her.

The gun clicked on empty. Lucy reached for it, grabbing it in her hand, the skeletal fingers closing over it and then tossing it aside.

The freaked out deputy grabbed the candle that sat near the side of the hole, just beyond where we'd tumbled in. He tossed it at her.

I watched as the skeletal apparition went up in flames, lighting the rest of the woods on fire.

"We need to go," I yelled, pulling the deputy out of the hole with me.

He climbed up easily, but then stood looking at the fire, glancing around, as if he were trying to decide if there was anything to fight the fire with.

The flames burnt through the dryer brush that been uncovered when the police started digging. I watched as they burned as high as my waist and then began to die down. Still, it moved easily through the brush, a sort of crawl rather than a large inferno. That began when the flames hit the first of the pines.

The deputy was still getting only static on the radio. I tugged at him and we began to run.

I hoped I was heading towards the rest stop. The purr of tires on pavement was drowned out by the crackle and hiss of the fire behind us. I was no longer cold. I was hot. The fire wasn't moving terribly quickly, eating through the first of the pines that had lived in the wooded area for years. It would pick up speed fast unless the dampness in the underbrush slowed it down. I hoped so. I hoped that the trees were soaked inside too.

The smoke grew thick and dark, trying to choke me. I felt like this was a last hurrah of Lucy, trying to choke me with the smoke. Perhaps she'd choked, though I thought she said she was beaten to death. I wouldn't know, not unless those bones were hers and I somehow persuaded the coroner to tell me.

I broke through the trees with the deputy. His radio still had some static, but he was able to call for fire fighters.

"What the hell was that?" he breathed, looking at me.

"I don't know. I think I saw her about twenty years ago here, the week before the woman was killed then. I think she was after me."

The deputy gave me a long hard look like he wondered if I was pulling his leg. But he'd seen Lucy. Seen that her ghost didn't react like it should have.

Ronette's car was across the parking lot. I hurried over there, suddenly terrified of what I might find, or now. What if Lucy had knocked her out and she was in the woods?

"Wait!" the deputy called.

"My friend's car. I don't see her," I yelled back, hoping he'd get the idea. I didn't know if he did but I heard the tap of his shoes on the asphalt when we ran.

The parking lot was getting a little smoky. It wasn't bad yet. Someone could have been having a barbecue. I looked in Ronette's car. She wasn't inside.

I looked around the area.

My eyes caught the restroom.

I hurried towards it.

As in a bad dream, I couldn't move fast enough. My chest was tight. I hoped she wasn't in there. I hoped that if she was, she was alive.

The lights were back on, though one of them flickered a bit. I bit back a gasp. It could have been normal, maybe.

I was through the door in seconds. Inside, the spilled salt. A shoe, attached to a foot. A body lying there, purple hair spread out around the salt.

A slight groan.

Red on the floor. Blood.

"Ronette?" I called softly, dreading that I'd touch her and she'd be dead.

Instead that slight groan again.

I went to her, feeling her head. No injuries there. The blood on the floor seemed to puddle but it wasn't so much that I thought she'd bled out. She could survive this, at least I hoped so.

The deputy had followed me in. He spoke into his radio calling for an ambulance as well as the fire trucks.

He went down and helped me roll her over. There was only a little blood. A thick white bone stuck out of her left side, as if someone had broken it off. For now, it was blocking whatever blood might flow.

"What happened?" I asked softly.

"She was there. And hit me in the stomach. It was like her hand went through my body," Ronette mumbled. "So hot..."

Ronette's head turned and her eyes lost focus. She was

still breathing but I didn't like the way sweat beaded on her forehead

My heart pounded. What had Lucy done? This was worse than if she killed me. If it were me and I died, it would just be over. I'd have failed, but I'd only have failed me. Tonight, I'd failed Ronette and her whole family could pay for it.

The room went foggy and my nose plugged. If the deputy was speaking to me, I didn't hear him. I was alone with my fears, my sorrows, and my anger at what had happened.

Someone came and started moving me away from Ronette. I wanted to stay but a woman in a uniform looked me in the eye and gestured that I should leave. I let her lead me out of the restroom.

She asked me questions I didn't understand, but another part of me answered them easily. She seemed satisfied with what I said. Outside, the smoke was thick enough to have some of the truckers getting out and walking around. Or maybe it was the red and blue lights that woke them. If there were sirens, the rushing in my ears kept me from hearing them.

Ronette was taken out on a gurney and the nice women in the uniform brought me to the same ambulance, settling me in while the other medic worked on Ronette. I worried about the rental car, about getting in contact with Ronette's family. I felt around, found my phone in my pocket. My purse was locked in the trunk of the rental car so if I needed ID that was going to be a pain.

I let it go, let myself drown in my worries about Ronette and Lucy.

I wondered if the fire had taken care of Lucy. Fire was supposed to be cleansing. I'd thought about lighting the rest stop on fire. Maybe her grave was better.

I didn't understand why had she attacked Ronette but didn't kill her.

Too many questions.

If those weren't enough, I worried about what the deputy would say when he reported finding me in the wood. I pushed that aside. Ronette was the only important worry in my life right then.

37

TRACI: SEPTEMBER NOW

Ronette woke the next day around noon. I'd found a number for her family and called it. I'd stuck around the hospital. I'd need a ride to my car eventually. Sheriff's deputies came by a couple of times and talked to me. I saw the young man from the woods once. He was sitting on a table as I was led out of the emergency area.

The lights were too bright even for me. The beeps and bells of machines and the squeak of wheels rolling down the tile hallways echoed around me. The place smelled like all hospitals, that chemical scent of bleach and sickness.

The sounds and lights didn't keep the worry away. I had so many questions, so many things that I needed to consider that when I finally got to a bathroom, the fact that I was alone in a strange restroom didn't phase me. Lucy didn't appear.

I waited in a waiting room to hear about Ronette. Her husband showed up with both girls later on. They looked as shook up as I felt. Her husband looked at me, seemed perplexed about whether he knew me or not, decided the not was easier. I didn't disabuse him of the notion. Having followed Ronette on Facebook, I recognized her girls.

She was going to be okay. I let the family go in first. It was nearly an hour later that the girls went out for something to eat. The husband came out and told me Ronette was asking for me.

I went in, cautiously. I wanted to cry.

"I'm so sorry," I said.

"You didn't ask me to go back," Ronette said. "I did that. I'm not sure I believed you, not really. Not in the way I should have. It was so weird. Lucy reached inside me, like she was going to gut me or something. Her hand got hot, like touching hot coals, and then she was gone, but the bone was still there. I think I passed out at the idea of it more than anything."

I nodded, sniffling. I couldn't speak.

"And then you were there with the deputy. The doctors were pretty weirded out about the bone. I guess it was old. Like someone dug up an old bone and stabbed me with it. The weird thing? I guess the fingers were curled around my spleen and none of them can figure that out."

I shuddered.

"What did you do?" Ronette asked.

"I thought you were with me in the woods," I said. "You said you'd come, and I went. I thought you were following me, but it was Lucy."

"I intended to follow you. But I was slow. Then when I got to the tree line, you insisted upon sending me back, that you needed to do this thing alone. So I went back to the car. I got tired of waiting and thought I'd use the bathroom. I'll know better than to do that again." There was a little laugh at that.

I was cold all over, not even certain what to say. Ronette asked me what happened.

I told her what I knew, down to the deputy throwing the candle towards Lucy as she had rushed him that last time.

"Do you think that's what made her stop, finally? Her resting place burned?"

"But her bones weren't there. Why would her resting place stop her?"

"Maybe the bones we found weren't hers," Ronette said. "Did you say that you'd read there were other bones found in the area? And you just said that Lucy told you a man had paid her sister to use her, probably to kill her. What if she wasn't the only girl he murdered? This could have been his burial area."

"So it's not just Lucy's ghost," I said. Did I need to lay them all to rest?

"Lucy was the one who was mad. She was the one who wanted revenge," Ronette said. She yawned, tired. I let her close her eyes and slipped out. I signaled to her husband and went in search of someone who could take me to the rest stop for my car.

The deputy from the woods was downstairs, waiting for me, drinking coffee. I asked how he knew I was there.

"Assignment," he said. "And because I'm supposed to be taking it easy after last night. Everyone thinks I'm frigging crazy, except maybe you because you were there."

"Unfortunately," I said.

"I didn't mention the candle. I only said something started the fire. Being near a crime scene isn't a crime to them. I couldn't say more because I'm not sure I'd be alive if you hadn't kept that thing away from me."

"I think there might be more bones there," I said.

"What makes you say that?" he asked.

"Just a feeling."

"Cause after the burn was out, this morning they went

and looked around and there were a half dozen more places bits of old bone sticking up. Like an old graveyard."

"Bet they were all missing women," I said. "Or maybe not. Maybe no one cared enough to miss them."

I could only hope that there was one set of bones that had been burned completely.

We drove in silence to my car. It was still where I'd parked. There were more police cars out there. I saw more movement in the woods. The stand was still there but thinner. Light came through it on the other side and the air smelled of burnt wood.

The deputy watched me unlock the trunk and get my purse. I'd lost the other stuff out in the fire but I didn't care. All I needed was my purse. I'd be in Portland before dark and spend my last night in the hotel. I had hoped to see Ronette today but she needed to rest. I hoped she'd be okay.

The drive was uneventful. I was more relaxed than I had been in some time. Things finally felt like something had changed, like I was free.

Although I felt as if I might need to use the restroom I passed the next rest stop without a second thought. There were limits to my sudden ease of fear.

The rain started as I got to Vancouver and it was coming down hard when I got into the parking lot of the hotel. I took my stuff inside and settled in. I wasn't terribly hungry but knew I should eat. I was closing the door before I realized I hadn't turned on all the lights.

It made me smile to think that I might be getting better.

TRACI: NOVEMBER NOW

Will invited me to join him and his friends for Thanksgiving and I was looking forward to it. It wasn't that I was suddenly enamored of my coworker, but he'd listened to my story, asked good questions, and let me process in a way no one else had. Not even Ronette. In some ways, once she was out of the hospital, she was worse than Anson, practically denying it had ever happened.

I was alone on the floor on Wednesday afternoon before Thanksgiving. Most people had gotten an early start. I'd done my shopping early and was set for the evening. I'd take the Lynx over to Will's the next day. He told me that as the newest member of the "gang", a group of about seven people he knew in the area, I didn't have to bring anything. I was still bringing a bottle of wine. It seemed wrong to show up with nothing.

I turned off my computer and left the building. There were a few people on the first floor but not many.

The next day, I got to Will's easily. The Lynx wasn't as

busy as I would have expected, though I watched plenty of cars waiting at traffic lights and stop signs. The city was busy with people all heading out to eat too much.

Perhaps picking up my hopeful mood, the blue sky was cloudless. Getting off at Will's stop, I had perhaps a quarter mile walk down a narrow street. The neighborhood was clearly older, but well-kept. Though I walked through shadows of buildings, none of them moved. None of them felt evil.

I sighed, smiling. For once I wasn't terrified and practically running because I was afraid of a ghost.

Still, I jumped when my phone buzzed with a message. I tried to laugh at myself but it sounded a bit off even to me. Around me, the apartments and condos all looked quiet, though it was nearly noon. I heard traffic from the main street but no cars drove down this one.

I looked at the text. Ronette. A happy Thanksgiving text with a picture of her and her daughter posed with a pie. Ronette looked thinner than she had and paler, her smile more strained. Still, she was alive, having Thanksgiving with her family. After what we'd been through, I couldn't expect that she wouldn't have changed. Look at how I had changed after both my confrontations with Lucy.

I sent back a quick response and continued my walk to Will's. He lived in a townhouse, a narrow building with a single car garage, perhaps twenty years old, at least. If older, it had been kept up spectacularly. The red brick was bright and colorful, the cream siding a nice contrast. Each of the townhouses looked almost the same, but Will's had a rather poorly drawn turkey that said, "Welcome Gang" on the front door.

I rang the bell and waited. Will answered. I gave him the wine. In the hallway in front of him was a big coat tree and he directed me to hand up my stuff. Shoes littered the wood floor, the shallow scratches suggesting laminate.

Just beyond was a door to a narrow half bath. Laughter came from the great room and kitchen. As I walked past the door to the bath, I heard a faucet drip. Just once.

AUTHORS NOTE

Driving down I-5, there are plenty of rest stops, but not one of them is called Steely Woods. Technically, I believe they're rest areas now but I stuck with the older form simply because it distanced anyone from believing I was describing any particular rest area.

Having driven down that stretch of freeway far too often from Portland to Tacoma or Seattle, I've stopped at every single stop. During the day, they're often manned by people with coffee and cookies, or they were pre-pandemic. At night, things get quieter and the stops get a little creepy, especially if you're traveling alone.

I've often wondered what could happen if I had to stop alone at a rest area. This book grew out of a short story I wrote about Traci's encounter.

I've never traveled from Charlotte to Raleigh on I-85, though I have lived in Charlotte. I've stopped at the rest area Traci and her companions passed near Concord, though I invented a second one not far away, just outside of Salisbury for Deborah to die in. I didn't want to taint a rest area with even an imaginary death.

Despite the fact that I know of no deaths or ghostly attacks, most experts warn that after dark, if you're traveling alone, it's better to stop at a staffed establishment like a gas station or fast food restaurant for a break than at a rest area. Ghosts might not be real, but human danger is always a possibility.

Bonnie Elizabeth could never decide what to do, so she wrote stories about amazing things and sometimes she even finished them.

While rejection stung her so badly in person, she spent most of her young life talking to cats and dogs rather than people, she was unusually resilient when it came to rejections on her writing, racking up a good number of them.

Floating through a variety of jobs, including veterinary receptionist, cemetery administrator, and finally acupuncturist, she continued to write stories.

When the internet came along (yes she's old), she started blogging as her cat, because we all know cats don't notice rejection. Then she started publishing.

Bonnie writes in a variety of genres. Her popular Whisper series is contemporary fantasy and her Teenage Fairy Godmother series is written for teens. She has been published in a number of anthologies and is working on expanding her writing repertoire.

She lives with her husband (who talks less than she does) and her three cats, who always talk back.

Stay in Touch